NINE LIVES

NINE LIVES

PROVIDENCE PARANORMAL COLLEGE BOOK NINE

D.R. PERRY

DISRUPTIVE IMAGINATION

LMBPN Publishing
PMB 196, 2540 South Maryland Pkwy
Las Vegas, NV 89109

Version 2.0 July, 2021
ebook ISBN: 978-1-64971-921-8
Print ISBN: 978-1-64971-922-5

CHAPTER ONE

Olivia

"So you understand, Doctor Watkins, that you must answer honestly." Mr. Ichiro folded his hands as he peered across his desk. "The prosecutor will try to derail the testimony we've discussed if you give her even the smallest chance. Your colleague's life is at stake here."

"I'm not letting some green DA bully me on the stand, Yoshi." A lopsided grin lifted the professor's still-too-thin lips. It might have shamed the Devil if such a being existed. "Brodsky will have plenty of reasonable doubt on his side."

"That's precisely what I thought you'd say, Nathaniel." Mr. Ichiro's eyes lit with a sparkle of humor I envied. I hadn't been able to muster anything in that particular emotional department. Not since the night we lost Tony.

I bent my head over the stenographer's notebook, a stream of inked markings flowing from the pen in my hand as I recorded their conversation. The Law Offices Of Dunstable and Ichiro had recording devices, of course, both the mundane and the magical kind. But I needed something to keep my hands busy, especially since I'd thrown out the medication that kept me up all day.

At first, going off all the Adderall and Strattera had been a profound experience. Questions about how I'd been living struck my thoughts like thunderbolts from on high. Was this how normal nocturnal people felt all the time? Did other owl shifters live on those medications or off them? Why did my parents think I had to be diurnal, anyway? I hadn't imagined that having this much energy was possible, and my brain was like a perpetual motion machine.

"Well, I suppose that's all we've got to cover for this meeting, Nathaniel." Mr. Ichiro stood up and held out his hand, bowing slightly at the waist.

"Gotcha." Professor Watkin's grin only got bigger and more mischievous. "We'll be leading the hootenanny in that courtroom, Yoshi. No doubt." He dropped me a wink and then shook with Mr. Ichiro. After he let go, he moved his hands to the grips on his wheelchair. It didn't budge. "I hate this blasted contraption."

"Don't hate the chair, hate the coma." Mr. Ichiro stepped around the desk and started toward the back of the wheelchair.

"Please, sir," said a voice from behind me, "allow me."

Albert, the son of the Dunstable half of the law firm, stood in the doorway. I'd almost forgotten he worked here part-time. Must have been nice, having an in besides good grades at the best Extrahuman Law firm in the tri-state area. Then again, Al was technically my packmate in Tinfoil Hat, just like Yoshi's daughter. I had an in, too, but didn't feel too comfortable using it. And I didn't know either Albert or Kim that well.

I watched Al wheel Professor Watkins out of the office and down the hall, listening to the professor's running snarky commentary about requiring a license to drive a wheelchair. It reminded me of something Tony might say. The hallway and Al and the professor in his chair blurred over in a nanosecond. I closed my eyes. The stenographer's pad fell off my lap. The chair by the desk, used by people who hadn't been in a coma for the better part of six months like Professor Watkins, creaked.

"Miss Adler, thank you for your help this evening." Mr. Ichiro reached down to the floor, then placed something flat and dry in my hands.

"You don't have to thank me, Mr. Ichiro." I curled my fingers around the rescued notebook. I opened my eyes and looked up at him. "Just doing my job."

"Under the circumstances, I'd expect you to work from your dormitory and transcribe the recordings." He gestured at the computer on his desk. My boss had a point. All the audio files went to the tablet he'd designated for my use during the internship we'd arranged.

"Circumstances?" I blinked.

"I'm sorry." Mr. Ichiro inclined his head. "Perhaps I presumed incorrectly, but I thought young Mr. Gitano was your mate."

"Um, no." I closed my eyes again, wishing I could just melt into a puddle on the floor like the Wicked Witch of the West after Dorothy gave her an impromptu shower. But I wasn't a witch at all, just a regular, plain old owl shifter who could see ghosts for some reason. But there was one ghost I hadn't laid eyes on, the most important one as far as I was concerned. Tony Gitano's. I opened my eyes, scanning the room just in case. Nope. Still no semi-transparent cat-man. I sighed. "We never got around to discussing that, sir."

"I see." My boss folded his hands together on the desk. "Should you need time to attend his memorial service, I will grant it."

"But what about the body, Mr. Ichiro? I think Tony might still—"

"Please, Miss Adler." The twinkle faded from Mr. Ichiro's eye, but nothing rolled down his cheek. "I understand that you have a unique perspective on the matter of young Mr. Gitano's demise." He leaned forward, lowering his voice. His eyes drifted to the open door behind me. "But whatever your belief, your attendance at the memorial is linked to a fortuitous outcome."

"Hoo, boy." I shook my head and matched his volume. "For whom?"

"You," Yoshi Ichiro's irises changed from their usual flat brown to rings of gold flecked with green. "Among others. Avoiding the memorial service could cause your Luck to take a turn for the worse." He returned to his chair, sitting up with his shoulders squared instead of leaning back. I realized he'd been checking on my Luck, something only Tanuki like Mr. Ichiro could do. "You ought to head back to your dorm and dress for that occasion before it's too late. I'll send you the files to transcribe later."

"Noted, sir."

"Oh, and please take this back with you as well." Mr. Ichiro handed me the intertwined bamboo stalks from his desk. I cradled the small glass container that sat in between my hands, then looked up at him. His eyes were bright but unfocused.

I opened my mouth, about to ask him for more information before he stopped scrutinizing whatever Luck energy happened to be around me. A floorboard creaked in the doorway at my back.

"Sorry if I'm interrupting." The floor creaked again. Under other circumstances, I might have turned around to see who was there. But I already knew by the voice and the apology. Henry Baxter, Psychic vampire. He was the Beta of the pack I belonged to, Tinfoil Hat. Also, he was the sole survivor of the killings Professor Brodsky stood accused of.

"Nothing to be sorry for, Henry." I stood and stepped aside, gesturing at the now empty chair. "I was just leaving, anyway."

"So you're going?" The vampire wasn't nearly as tall as the

other guys in Tinfoil Hat and, on the surface, nowhere near as intimidating unless he showed his fangs. He wore his ever-present black leather jacket over black slacks and a collarless black dress shirt. The Alliance Medallion that made his place in the pack so groundbreaking hung just over the third button. Henry had been the first vampire to join a wolf shifter pack since before the Big Reveal when everyone in the known universe found out about extrahumans. A handful of old vamps, worried that changes would destroy their covert power, had outed their wolfish allies and gone on a turning spree, ruining things for others. His hand on my shoulder snapped me out of my reverie with cold comfort. "You'll be at Tony's memorial?"

"Yeah." I shrugged, shaking his hand off my shoulder.

"You sure?" His eyebrows lifted.

"It's for the best if I go." I waved one hand at my powder-blue and slate-gray office attire. "But I've got to change if I want to fit in."

"Understood." Henry stepped to the other side of the chair I'd recently vacated, leaving me a clear path to the door.

As I walked out, I heard Henry mention a memory charm he'd found, something that he couldn't remember getting. It hadn't been in the bank box where he usually kept those things. Instead, it had been in his apartment.

"And I can't decipher any of the impressions I'm getting from it, Mr. Ichiro. It's like watching videos of toddlers playing. In the Under."

"Peculiar. But unless it pertains to Mr. Brodsky's trial, I'm sure it won't hurt to let its purpose come to light as coincidence dictates."

The idea of a Psychic equivalent of home videos intrigued me. I'd had no such thing until I got adopted at age four. Nothing I'd tried had revealed memories of my birth parents, or even where I'd lived before New Jersey. At least my parents had been as honest about my origins as their knowledge allowed. But there wasn't time to turn around and ask Henry whether his powers would help me or ask my boss why I needed lucky bamboo. Because I had to get out.

I escaped.

I had to put on just about every article of black clothing I owned to look funeral-appropriate. I'd worn exactly the same thing to Mr. Harcourt's Mourning Day a half year earlier, but somehow, I'd lost the black handbag I'd used back then. All my usual must-haves went into a little black backpack instead because carrying my navy blue work bag would have looked all wrong. I couldn't help but care even though the last thing I wanted to do in this world was to attend a memorial service for a man I love. Loved. No, that was wrong.

The night his dad signed the DNR order, I thought he might still be alive. And I still did, despite all the evidence to the contrary and my own usual tendency to stick with the simplest explanation. The doctor had pronounced time of death, and an interrupted autopsy had determined the cause (copper dagger fragment adjacent to the left ventricle). And the minute the medical examiner turned his back, Tony's body had up and vanished.

I glanced over my shoulder at Mr. Ichiro's bamboo on my desk before opening the door to stride down the hall toward the elevator. I'd already questioned Margot Malone's imp friend and Gee-Nome about Tony's missing body.

Both pure faeries were capable of instantly transporting something Tony's size. I owed the imp big-time by asking thrice, but it hadn't had anything to do with Tony's disappearance. And Gee-Nome had an alibi. Bianca Brighton. Either of them would have shown up on the morgue's security camera. I pushed the button and tapped my foot thirty-seven times until the elevator yawned emptily before me.

Even Umbral magic couldn't have gotten him out of there under the ME's nose. The camera would have blanked out, and a simple faerie glamour would have shown a shimmer on the recording. There were exactly two faeries who had the kind of power it'd take to get a body out without a trace, and I doubted the Goblin King or the Sidhe Queen had any interest in Tony Gitano. I'd seen a tiny blip of blue light, but no Magus or faerie could cast a spell that color. Only one type of extinct magical shifter could. My eyes were sharp, and I'd watched that footage so many times I owed Detective Weaver a year's supply of coffee.

I stepped into the elevator and imagined it swallowing my agitation like I used to down Adderal. The mystery of where Tony was now sat tangled in the corners of my mind. I couldn't cut through that knot and had no further ideas on how to tease out answers. Someone had pushed all the buttons on the way up to the fifth floor. My hands curled into fists, my fingernails pressing against the calluses in my palms. The doors opened on the fourth floor.

It was a fact that the Extramagus, Richard Hopewell, tried to kill Bianca and Tony and me all at the same time. What made things worse was, even if we traced the magic in the explosion that brought the Olneyville house literally down, he could claim he got paid to do some wards that went up by accident. Tony's father could show registry documents, and both he and Hopewell would get off Scot-free. But we all knew better. Tony had told us so.

No one besides me bothered listening to him most of the time. He'd sauntered in the front door of that house while I busted through the attic window. I'd heard him downstairs even though Bianca couldn't in her diabetic stupor. Tony had argued

with his Dad's wise guy about how the place would go up, definitely on purpose, no accidentally about it. But my testimony
wouldn't do much against Tony's father. Two people telling the
same story on the stand would have been a game-changer, but
Bianca had been out cold at the time and hadn't heard a thing. I
rolled my eyes, waiting for the doors to close on the third floor.

The others believed Tony was dead. They didn't want to listen
to little old strung-out me. Except I wasn't on meds anymore.
They didn't understand the difference it made, how all the facts
came into relentless focus. Gino Gitano had spoken to me right
after they called the time of death. I'd swallowed my rage in the
face of Gino's smug cordiality after watching his son die, something that felt unreal in my heart even though my brain knew
better. Tony never came out and said it directly, but that night
confirmed my worst speculations. The danger I'd suspected he
lived in on a near-constant basis had been real all along.

It's easy to hear about something like that without understanding when you come from a family like mine. My parents
always said they wanted me so badly, they went to court. For
someone whose parents chose me to love from a crowd of
orphans, Tony's situation seemed like part of a vigilante's origin
story.

Maybe life under such an intimate and constant threat was
the reason Tony had gone so far out of his way every time he
found his friends in danger. And now, I was the one in Richard
Hopewell's cross-hairs. I wouldn't delude myself into thinking
he'd let up on me now. On the second floor, a pair of hirsute
Freshmen blinked, then backed off under my glare. And I
couldn't blame them for choosing the stairs over an elevator ride
with an angry owl shifter.

I wouldn't believe Tony Gitano was dead. I also couldn't
believe he'd made himself scarce deliberately. Not when I was the
one in danger. He'd saved me twice before, once when I crashed
into the side of a house to help Henry and Maddie, and after that,

he'd gotten me out of the tentacles of a magipsychic construct before it could crush me. And then it had been my turn to look out for him. I jumped through hoops so he could become an informant with Newport PD and helped him evade Richard while he kept Fred Redford's faerie cap out of his hands. The elevator chime sounded, but the doors took their sweet time opening on the ground floor.

My fist hit wood as I punched the inside of the elevator. I wasn't in mourning. Instead, I was in a state of slowly burning rage. Going to this memorial felt like a waste of time. I should be out turning over more leaves, looking for more clues. Since Luck dictated I should go anyway, the fire in my belly would have to wait. Any advantage in the Luck department could get negated in an instant if I flew off the handle, literally or figuratively.

My ballet flats slapped against pavement after I pushed through the doors to the vestibule and hit the sidewalk outside. I didn't give a fluff of down how my anger looked, either. I crossed the street, heading toward my car in the parking lot in a straight line.

People thought the SmartCar suited me. It didn't. Mom had picked it out according to *her* sensibilities. She was human and didn't really understand shifters even though she tried. I only vaguely remembered that day at the dealership where she and Dad always bought their own efficient sedans, nodding at the salesman. His tie had been silvery blue, almost the same color as the car I drove off the lot two weeks before heading up from New Jersey to Providence Paranormal College.

It'd been a long strange series of trips since then, oddly cloudy but brightly lit at the same time. This spring, something inside me cracked open, breaking in past the pane of shelter my parents had raised me behind. The shards and dust of that cataclysm finally settled this semester, revealing the world in sharper focus once Mr. Ichiro had put me on the night shift and gotten me off the diurnal drug cocktail.

Clipping the seatbelt around me felt like an automatic artifact of my old life on the meds. A thread of rage, sudden and hot as a solar flare, rose up within me. I'd bent and caved to the rules for as long as I could remember, and if I didn't try to do things differently now, maybe I'd never get the chance. I closed my eyes and reached for the belt, defying Rhode Island law and damning the torpedoes by unbuckling it.

Someone knocked on the passenger side window.

I screamed, the screech absorbed by drab fabric upholstery. My head turned at an unnatural-for-humans angle, but the figure peering in the window didn't startle or turn to run away. Of course not. He was a dragon. The middle finger of my left hand pressed a button, and the window lowered. The door stayed locked.

"What do you want, Blaine?"

"Um, I was hoping I could get a ride over to the memorial instead of the owl death stare?"

"What did you expect, anyway? And why in the world would you want to mourn Tony Gitano?" I tucked my chin, widening my eyes as I felt my hair tumble around my face. Stupid owl posturing instincts. I wasn't used to subverting them like Jeannie, Kim, or Bobby because the meds used to take the screech out of my owl for me. "You always acted like you hated the guy."

"Look, I was wrong, okay?" Blaine ducked his head but didn't break eye contact with me. Silly dragon. He didn't know that staring contests are for owls.

"Would have been nice if you'd realized that last week." I kept my gaze on him, unblinking, and waited. "Anyway, you're a billionaire. Don't you have a car you can call?"

"It's full of everyone else." Blaine looked down at his shoes and shuffled his feet. I'd expected him to roll his eyes instead of flopping like a deflated football. When he spoke next, his voice stayed low and even instead of reminding me of a pebble in a shoe. "I thought it was more important that they go than me."

That did it. I pressed the button again, watching the window rise between me and the dragon shifter. After that, I flipped the switch to unlock the door, then looked straight ahead through the windshield until Blaine got in.

After that, I fastened my seatbelt like a good girl and pointed the nose of the silver SmartCar at Swan Point Cemetery.

CHAPTER TWO

Olivia

The sky had no business being impeccably clear over Swan Point Cemetery, the stars twinkling too mirthfully for such a somber occasion. I stalked across the lawn toward the Hope Memorial Garden, stopping at the fringes of a group in front of the Fishman sculpture there. I stared up, blinking as the early moonlight emphasized the narrow space between two triangular monoliths that framed an old anchor. It was red-brown, nearly the same color as Tony's unshifted eyes. I couldn't believe I'd never see them again.

I crossed my arms over my chest, waiting to see what kind of ceremony the Gitano family could possibly have without a body to bury. Bianca Brighton turned around, then put a hand on my shoulder. I let her. She glanced past me once and nodded, then directed her attention back to me. She said nothing.

I didn't blame her.

Bianca had spent most of the week between that damn explosion and this ridiculous service trying to convert me to her ideology of what had happened to Tony. She thought the Extramagus had tossed him into the Under before his ghost could detach from his body. That'd trapped him in there so he couldn't tell us any secrets he knew. Ghosts from here couldn't travel to and from the Faerie realm, and the queen had put a ban on any medium traveling in her side of the realm without her direct invitation and supervision. Bianca had neither of those things, so her theory remained unproven.

That was fine by me. I didn't believe it anyway.

People in the pack knew only that Tony was a shifter of the housecat variety and the underwhelming son of an overbearing crime lord. I knew a bit more than they did. Tony Gitano was a liar and a thief and an escape artist. He also had a code and loyalty to his friends. I'd seen him get Josh Dennison out of his house only seconds ahead of a rival werewolf pack sent there to detain him. He'd dodged pure faeries and an Extramagus for twenty-three hours to keep Fred Redford safe. He'd played informant to detectives while convincing wise guys he wasn't a rat to help Blaine in the spring and Lane over the summer. I'd fallen on a trampoline he'd managed to hide in plain sight on a side street in Olneyville. Alone.

So I believed in that surly neighborhood cat-man, and I couldn't envision him doing anything but evading death. Most of the time I logicked things more than Mr. Spock, but not this. Not Tony being dead when his body had up and vanished in the middle of his autopsy without any alterations on the security camera.

Maybe the reason anger plagued my gut instead of grief was just part of my personal process. I glanced around, noticing the motley assembly of my Tinfoil Hat packmates. Blaine hadn't been kidding about no room in his limousine, it brought his mate, Kim, Bobby and Lynn, Josh and Nox, Henry and Maddie, Jeannie and Ismail, Lane and Margot, and Bianca with her ghost companion Horace. I noticed Josh's sister Beth Dennison turning her back on Ren Ichiro, the son of my boss who'd ended up with a Selkie pelt somehow. Everyone had thought Ren was dead, too, yet there he was, pissing his ex-fiancée off just by existing. The child prodigy, Psychic medium Ed Redford, was there, chaperoned by YouTube famous Empathy Psychic Irina Kazynski.

I stopped, not wanting to push past the larger-than-expected crowd, including the rest of the vampires in Lane's band, Night Creatures. Even their rival at the Battle of the Bands, Jack Steele, stood off to one side with his newly vamped fiancée Della clinging to his arm. I turned my head, blinking as I realized just how many people cared about Tony. He wouldn't see it that way, of course. He'd think all these people were just that fed up with the Extramagus, and his death was the last straw.

Off to the other side, I recognized a few more familiar faces. Gemma Tolland and her grandfather, both Unseelie trolls who'd rescued a few of my packmates, stood at a slight distance from the rest of the group. They chatted amiably with Neil Redford, a Redcap Duke in the Goblin King's court. The dragon librarian, Taki Waban, stood stiff and formal alongside Headmistress Henrietta Thurston, whose eyes were puffy and rimmed with red.

A crunch of recently frosted-over grass underfoot announced a new set of arrivals. I wasn't happy to see them. All the same, Gino Gitano gave me his best smile. I recognized it from the numerous press photos of him on courthouse steps after each of his dismissed cases. In those newsprint front-page portraits, he was never alone. The same held true here, though instead of lawyers in Brioni suits, he had bruisers in Belvedere with one exception.

Gino Gitano was a widower and didn't keep female company as far as anyone could tell. Except on this, the night of his son's funeral, there was a woman on his arm. She was young, maybe my age. Wavy, bobbed, black hair, so glossy it might have been a wig, framed an oval face with olive skin and glinting gray eyes that seemed to look past everything. Her bony hand rested on

Mr. Gitano's broad forearm like a sparrow might pause on a bare autumn branch. Her body looked less frail, her figure more filled out than I remembered it being the year before. She'd definitely put on weight.

"Cassandra," whispered Bianca. I glanced at her and understood. Everyone on campus knew about Cassandra Spanos, the Psychic who'd created a weather app and distributed it for free last fall at Freshman orientation. Tony's dad had a Precognitive Psychic working for him. Cassandra had freaked out about something, given Lynn a special version of her app, and then mysteriously vanished from PPC about a year ago. Well, inexplicably to us, anyway. I was sure she had plenty of her own reasons. At any rate, she didn't look happy about escorting her employer. Or whatever he was to her.

And that's when I saw the last thing I expected. Off to one side of the anchor sculpture, where the most moonlight fell, I watched three figures step forward, as though through a doorway of light made of thin air. One of these had a chalky, gray skin and sandy hair topped with a Pawtucket Red Sox cap, Fred Redford, the newest Seelie knight at the Sidhe Queen's court. To his left stood a figure taller even than his six foot two inches. Her hair was like the ruddy rays of dawn with noontime highlights, her skin clear as morning dew. Her features and stance held a chaste beauty that no one would think to ascribe to any being her age.

I blinked, puzzled by the presence of the Sidhe Queen. The ruler of the Under's daylight realm and monarch of all things Seelie had nothing to do with Tony, but I realized that she wasn't here because of him when I noticed who stood at her left. Richard Hopewell, the Extramagus. He looked directly at Cassandra Spanos and smiled.

I watched Gino caress her arm as she shuddered under Richard's creepy grin, not realizing I'd done the same until I saw her get the response under control. I kept right on shaking though, this time with anger. A tear trickled down my left cheek. Here was another of my classmates, manipulated by Hopewell and worse off than the rest of us or it. Except Cassandra was alone and packless. She'd been singled out before the rest of us had any idea what was going on. No wonder Hopewell and the Gatto Gang always seemed one step ahead of us. They'd had a Psychic in their pockets all that time.

"Friends of my son's," said Gino. My attention snapped back to the man who'd brought us all here to mourn while he gloated. I knew he was more relieved than sad, happier to have a dead son than a prison sentence.

"Yeah, unlike you," I murmured under my breath. Every shifter in my vicinity held theirs, and every vampire froze. I set my jaw, the comment not even remotely an accidental foot-in-mouth blurt. I'd meant every word, and then some.

Gino Gitano's gaze met mine, our glares clashing like low- and high-pressure fronts. A storm brewed between us, but neither of us knew how much damage it'd do before it resolved. If it ever did. I had no way or means to stand up to someone as powerful or connected as the Gatto boss. Safe for now, he cleared his throat.

"Everyone here cared about my Tony. Some of you, I imagine, might even have loved him to death." Gino didn't blink. Neither did I, even though it rained on my face as it always did when I got angry. "I hope that this service helps all of us finally find peace, even though someone...special...is forever absent from our lives. This anchor behind me..." Gino waved one hand, gesturing at the sculpture. "This anchor is a symbol of hope, one which will—"

I felt a gust of chill air and almost heard a voice from off to my left tell me to cool it. So I tore my eyes away from Gino to look in that direction. I was just in time to see the last of the guests arrive.

Instead of light, this was a portal into darkness. One figure materialized from it, a long, black coat in silhouette. I blinked.

Could it be Tony? The tears stopped, and my heart fluttered like some caged thing beating against bars, desperate to be free. I took a step forward, but a hand clamped down on my right wrist. A fanged visage framed by green hair invaded my field of vision.

"Hey, Olivia." Lane Meyer tapped his nose with his free hand. "Sniff before you leap."

"Oh." My nostrils flared, catching the scent of something ancient and ragged like an old ballgown pulled from a steamer trunk unopened for centuries. As I turned to look again at the last guest, I understood. The coat wasn't a black trench, but a long-tailed tux, silver frills foaming up at the figure's neck like Arctic sea foam. It wasn't Tony, late to his own memorial. I was looking at the Goblin King, the monarch of Unseelie faeries.

A face peeked out from behind the ragged hem of the king's coat. They had bushy gray brows above twinkling eyes, and their smile displayed teeth made of seashells. Gee-Nome, Henry Baxter's pure faerie pal, waggled those eyebrows at me like Groucho Marx. Gee dropped me a wink I couldn't return. Instead, I rolled my eyes and looked at the Goblin King's face.

The king's expression seemed placid instead of somber, as I might have expected. It called to mind the stillness of an autumn dusk after a cold snap had silenced summer's insects. He actually caught my eye and tilted his head at me, a gesture of respect so unexpected that I almost turned to see if someone more esteemed, like Mr. Ichiro or Hertha Harcourt, stood behind me. I could only think of one reason I'd merit his notice. I'd put myself squarely in Mr. Hopewell's crosshairs by helping to rescue Bianca.

Maybe I shouldn't have been surprised at the king's display of respect. He'd intervened on behalf of our mismatched pack before. No one would say why, but I thought Richard, the Extramagus throwing in his lot with the Sidhe Queen, a likely reason. I glanced at her, unable to imagine how she'd ever been the king's wife back in the days when the world was new. It made total sense to me that they'd broken up. Opposites attract, but they rarely maintain proximity for long.

"Please continue, Gino Gitano." The Goblin King didn't tilt his head at Tony's dad. Didn't even bother to look down his nose at him.

"I was talking about symbols of hope. My son was one." The social slight wasn't lost on Gino. I watched the pupils of his eyes elongate and go catlike, his anger palpable. Still, I had to give him credit for continuing his interrupted speech, mainly because he pitched the next part directly at me. "He saved lives, and even with his loss, that fact remains to this day. Symbols of hope are things that even when you don't want to hold on, they cling to you. They pull you to destinations beyond anything you'd imagine or dare to desire for yourself."

I knew a threat when I heard one. I turned, intending to walk back across the cemetery to my car, regardless of Luck. Something cold and clawed had me by the ankle. I looked down to find that seashell smile.

"Hello, Gee." I shook my head, then sighed. "And goodbye. I've gotta go."

"No, not yet." The Gnome's eyes moved slowly to the left and then to the right. "You want to know why."

"Not enough to flat-out ask you, Gee." I tried to lift my leg to take the next step away from the sans-body mockery of a funeral, but the Gnome had too firm a grip. "Hoo, boy. Let go already."

"Aww, you're no fun." Gee clinging to my ankle like that reminded me of Gino's ominous anchor analogy. "But stay a while. His Majesty wants words with you."

"Wait, what?" I blinked, then let out a groan of frustration as I realized I'd asked the Gnome a question. Two more, and I'd be on the hook to him for a favor. That was how it was with any faerie creature except the shifters.

"Yes, little...hmm. Owl. Yes, that's what you appear to be. The

Goblin King attended in the hope you'd be here." Gee jerked their chin at Gino, twinkling eyes rolling.

"And of course, you're waiting for me to ask why." I felt my mouth curl into a smirk despite my foul mood. The steady drone of Gino Gitano's overthought and underplayed funerary act fell to the wayside of my consciousness.

"Of course," mimicked the Gnome. They winked. That simple gesture by the vertically challenged faerie creature lifted my spirits like an updraft. I did the most natural thing in the world, as instinctive as the impulse to sleep during the day.

I laughed.

Everyone and everything around me went silent. Even the crickets stopped chirping. I looked up, ignoring Gino's inevitable glare as I scanned the crowd for any hint of support or even sympathy. Nothing.

The silence broke and voices carried, mostly murmurs questioning either my empathy or my coping skills. A few doubted my sanity because, of course, mated shifters commonly denied the death of their other halves. But I hadn't been Tony's mate, and if I was crazy, it was for believing he still lived. I looked down again to find Gee smiling up at me. That smile made of seashells was creepy but more reassuring than the ocean of doubt around me. The Gnome glanced at someone, so I followed his gaze.

"Miss Adler." The Goblin King stood half an arm's length from me, his hand extended in my specific direction. "Please allow me to escort you to your vehicle."

"Of course, Your Majesty." I gave him the best curtsy I could manage with a Gnome hanging from my right calf. Then, I held my hand out toward his palm up.

The king didn't grasp my hand. Instead, he lowered his until just the tips of our fingers touched. I felt a twinge of magic and furrowed my brow until my legs started moving on their own. They matched his steps out of the crowd and away from the memorial sculpture in perfect synchrony. Magical procession march. Interesting. I felt more than one glare glance across my back and realized I'd just made an enemy besides Gino Gitano. The Sidhe Queen. None of my friends could say I did things by small measures after that.

"Your Majesty is too kind, ushering me away from the scene of my own bad manners." The indignant fire in my belly flared again, this time with a desire to know what business a Faerie monarch could have with little old me.

"You bear a striking resemblance to your mother, did you know that?" The king smiled down at me.

All the hair on the nape of my neck stood on end. At first, I thought, why should I freak out? It's no secret that I'm adopted. But then I wondered. Had the Goblin King known my birth mom? I'd be willing to owe him the world if only he'd tell me about her.

"Um, Your Majes—"

"Please, call me Ron."

"Wow, that's an unexpected honor. Thank you." I wrestled my jaw closed. "Ron. I'd never have guessed that was your given name."

"It's just one I go by on occasion." A smile played at the corners of the king's lips, as ragged as the hem of his tuxedo. I got the impression he didn't get to use that expression as much as he'd like. "I understand you're petitioning the mortal courts on behalf of the Summoner Pavlo Brodsky. Is this correct?"

"Yes."

"Good. I want you to stop."

"Um, I'm not sure I can." I sighed. "It wouldn't make a difference anyway. The trial will go on without one intern."

"It's not the trial I'm concerned with, but your freedom from participation in it. I've got a situation in the Under, in my demesne. There's a creature who is there without my permission.

That cannot be. Your attention to that matter is of greater importance than this mortal court's trial."

"Look, Ron," I turned my head, relying on the king's magic to keep me moving without making me trip over my own feet. I almost reminded him that I wasn't one of his tithed subjects or even a faerie creature, but that felt wrong for some reason I couldn't name. The instinct that failed to stop my laughter earlier got my tongue surely as a cat. "I signed on as an intern for Mr. Ichiro before you made this request, and he expects my help." I paused, thinking about how to explain internships for college credit to a Faerie monarch. "It's a contract I've made with the school and Mr. Ichiro, you see."

"Does this contract ban you from leaving the mortal realm?"

"Well, no, but it bans me from deserting my obligations." I sighed. "I have to be there tomorrow because I need to write a paper on the experience for my grade. So I'm sorry, Ron, but I can't skip out on it."

"Then don't." The king stopped his processional march as we reached the silver SmartCar. My magically-propelled feet took two more steps, then turned me so I faced him. "I will expect you at my hunting lodge twenty-four hours from now. You will be given a weapon, assistance, and a dossier on your quarry."

"As long as I have a way to get there, I'll show up." I nodded once, entirely unclear about how I'd use a weapon in owl form. Only magical shifters got to keep any semblance of a humanoid form in the Under.

"Thank you, Messenger." His words sounded like a title though his smile made me question any gravity it might have. The king bowed his head again.

"Um, you're welcome, I guess." I sat on the most urgent of the army of nagging questions our conversation had inspired.

"Gee-Nome," The king crooked one finger, and the Gnome let go of my leg.

"Your Majesty!" Gee bowed so low, his nose brushed the asphalt.

"You will keep an eye on Olivia Adler. Ensure she comes to no harm and secure her passage at the proper time."

"Yes, Great King!"

The monarch occasionally known as Ron walked backward, a gust of autumnal wind blowing ragged tux tails toward me as he went. He melted into darkness, the reverse process of how he'd made his entrance beside the sculpture. The last I saw of him that night was his grin, as wide and bright as that cat from Cheshire.

I got in my car, fastened the seatbelt, and drove off. I didn't worry about driving Blaine back to campus. He could hail himself a Lyft or Uber. I understood his ride request had actually been about giving that long-overdue apology.

"Hoo, boy! I forgot Gee," I said into the flow of warm recycled air coming from the defrost vents.

"Can't forget me," the Gnome said from the passenger seat. I managed not to jump.

Back at the dorm, I didn't pass Go or collect two hundred dollars. I just flailed my way into pajamas and flopped into bed. Sleep came for me faster than a Gnome could vanish.

CHAPTER THREE

Olivia

I woke up at a quarter past noon and lay in bed, blinking up at the ceiling. I still had my old alarm clock, the one loud enough to wake me in the morning during my time as a day creature. It had an LED projector that lit the ceiling up like a temporal Borealis with digitally inscribed hours and minutes in block numerals.

The clock would have let me sleep for three more hours. This was the earliest I'd risen all semester. My internal clock and rhythms were messed up since I'd gone to bed at an unusual time. I rolled over, trying to ignore the blue-green numbers and the heaviness that meant I'd need to get to the restroom soon, but something was off. Instead of drifting back to sleep as originally intended, I flung the blankets away and sprang off the bed, landing in a defensive crouch.

"Don't get your feathers in a ruffle." The little figure who spooked me tucked most of their squat body behind the monitor on my desk.

"Geez, Gee." I lowered my arms. "It's not nice to startle someone when she's sleeping."

"Didn't." The Gnome eyed me warily. "Woke and spooked yourself, you did."

"Whatever, Yoda." I shifted my weight from one foot to the other. "Don't touch anything until I get back." I grabbed my basket of toiletries and headed out the door and down the hall to the fifth-floor bathroom. I stowed everything under a bench, out of the way of anyone else who might come in.

In the shower, I tried to imagine washing away all the turmoil I'd felt in the week since the fire in the house in Olneyville. I shut my eyes, attempting to sort through my thoughts of words and images. That didn't work out so well for me.

Events from the previous week flashed across the backs of my eyelids like a movie trailer on a silver screen, except in slow motion. Tony sailed through the air, missing the trampoline Bianca and I had fallen on. I caught the glint of orange from the streetlight on his copper dagger this time. Falling from three stories wasn't guaranteed to kill a shifter, not even a relatively small one like Tony, but he'd fallen with a dagger made from his bane metal sticking out of him. That knife was as fatal to cat shifters as silver is to werewolves.

"No." My legs buckled under me, doubt smiting me. Could I be wrong? Was my faith in Tony simply denial? The water from the shower stung my skin too much, so I shut it off. After that, I couldn't move. The chill in the water felt like the icy grip of death. The door creaked on its hinges, exchanging tattered remnants of water vapor for the cold, dry air in the hallway.

"I don't get it." I couldn't identify the voice with the bathroom's echo, but it sounded familiar. "Like a lot of stuff about feelings and how people express them. Facts are facts, right?"

"Can you blame her?" The door punctuated the second woman's voice. "Well, maybe you can't. You might have a mate, but you're not a shifter. You don't know what it's like."

"So explain." With the door closed, I realized Lynn Frampton was the first speaker.

"There's no one way to explain it," the second woman said. "It's different for everyone. When it happened to me, I refused to believe it, too. I tried so hard to sense him, I started hallucinating. Hearing his voice, thinking I saw him. I limped all the way from my house across town to Federal Hill because I thought I smelled him one night, but Ren was gone."

"But Beth, Ren was actually alive all that time." I heard the faucet turn and the sound of running water, then splashing. "What if you weren't hallucinating?"

"There's no way." Beth Dennison's sigh bounced off the tile like a trapped sparrow. "Ren wasn't anywhere near me back then. Also, his scent changed after he took up the pelt, and more than that. So much is different about him, I'm not even sure if he's my mate anymore. As far as I'm concerned, he may as well have been dead all these years."

"So, should Olivia just give up?"

"That's too much judgment even for my taste." I heard a faint click and caught a whiff of something chalky, probably some kind of makeup. "She's the one living her life, not me. But I think Olivia's setting herself up for disappointment, whether Tony's dead or not. If they were mates, and he somehow survived, they might not be compatible anymore. Ask any Psychic or Undeath Magus. Surviving what should kill changes a person forever."

"I hope you're wrong." I heard Lynn sigh. "Come on. We'll be late for class. I can't believe you talked me into that Extrahuman Entertainment elective."

The door creaked again. Open, then closed. After a while, I could move again and stretched my legs out in front of me. My needled limbs reminded me of slow starts. That was how things had been between Tony and me until he put his foot on the brakes. I closed my eyes, remembering that seemingly endless party at the Dennison place five months earlier. I could almost hear his voice.

"So, what did you want to talk about?" Tony had stayed in the shadows, leaning against the old stone wall at the border of the back lawn.

"I just, um, wanted to see how you're doing." I hadn't moved closer to him at that point. Standing in the late-afternoon sunlight helped me stay awake even during day's hours. Moving into the half-light at his side might have cost me the ability to stay conversational. And I was nervous. There was that back then, too.

"Really?" He'd turned his head to peer at me from the corner of his eye instead of straight on. My cheeks had flushed with heat.

"It's a party, Tony." I'd blinked, wishing I didn't wear my emotions so openly in any situation that had to do with him. "Everyone else is off doing party things, not hiding in a hedge."

"I'm not everyone else." He'd faced me head-on that time but avoided locking gazes with me.

"I know." And I should have said more than that, but my courage was as dry as the Sahara back then.

"So why bother?" He crossed his arms over his chest.

"Because I care," I remember fixing my gaze on him, staring until he'd had no choice but to lock gazes with me.

"You shouldn't." He hadn't blinked, so I'd gotten to watch the pupils in his hazel eyes go vertical for a moment. Something about that confrontation had called to his cat side's instincts.

"I'm stubborn." The left corner of my mouth had curled up, unintentionally. He'd licked his lips, but then stopped himself and pressed them into a flat, thin line.

"I know." He'd leaned back against the ivy-covered wall behind him, closing his eyes and breaking the flow of whatever energy had gone between us. "Stubborn people get hurt. I ain't letting that kind of thing happen to you."

"You're worth the risk."

"I'm not."

"I'll be the judge of that."

"Look, I'm not here to party. I'm here for a reason, a favor I've gotta pay back before things get heavier than they already are. It's serious business."

"Then let me help."

"No."

"Why not? I've done it before."

"Yeah, I know. We saved Henry, and you almost got eaten by a Grim."

"But you kept me safe. And then you do stupid things like asking why I care and why I'm here." I'd swayed, weight shifting from my left foot to my right.

"And I still ask because so far, you haven't come out and told me the real reason a chick like you gives a damn about a cat like me." I wasn't exactly sure how he managed to fade into the shadows even more, but that's what had happened.

"For someone so vague and secretive, you sure love being on the receiving end of a straight answer." I'd put my hands on my hips and stepped all the way up to the line on the grass, that divide between the fading sunlight and full shadow.

"Yeah, so why don't you be a pal and lay one on me?"

"Tony, no one survives alone. That's the reason this whole pack got started in the first place. And you notice everyone's pairing off." I'd dropped my arms, wringing my hands.

"Yeah, I know. I think maybe that's not such a good idea unless the timing's exactly right."

"Time is what you make of it." I'd taken a deep breath and stepped into the darkness and across Tony's figurative line in the sand, too. "I'm seizing the moment."

"Wait, what?" Tony's eyes had widened as I stepped closer to him, and then our lips met. Diurnal me was always a clumsy creature. I'd stubbed my toes against his and stepped back with some mumbled apology.

We'd stood there blinking at each other for forever and a nanosecond at the same time. The world came apart and went back together again. Tony's eyes had gone feline and he'd pressed himself against me like metal to a magnet, tilting his head to kiss me back more thoroughly than I'd dared. And even with the black-hole gravitational inevitability between us, he'd somehow found the strength to push me away, saying "not yet."

Back in the present, I got my feet under me and stood. I had no idea whether Tony and I had been mates, but probably we were. If Beth was right, it didn't matter now, anyway. All the hope I'd fed and watered over the week curled up, shriveled and crispy-brown like that poor philodendron I'd neglected back in middle school. I threw my nightgown over my head, not caring that my hair soaked through the flannel, and shuffled into the hall. A group of people blocked the way to my room. I didn't bother looking up at them until one spoke.

"O-Olivia?" Lynn's hands went to her reddening cheeks. "You were in there while we—" Her face went to the other extreme, color making a quick exit to leave her pale. "I'm so sorry. And Beth's sorry, too."

"No way." Beth shook her head, sensibly bobbed hair bouncing to emphasize her denial. "I'm not. No one else should waste her time and make the mistake I did over Ren."

"But look at her, Beth; she's grieving." Kimiko Ichiro tugged at Beth's sleeve. "We both know what that's like. Show a little love."

"Yeah, but there's a piece you don't understand." Beth shrugged Kim off. "This is love. Tough love. We don't have time to mope or hope. After all this," Beth gestured at her prosthetic leg, which she'd lost in the accident that had almost killed Ren, "I didn't have both the Gatto Gang and Richard Hopewell out for my blood. Olivia does."

"I'd say that means she needs sympathy more than ever." Lynn put her hands on her hips, narrowing her eyes at Beth.

"No." Beth turned to face Lynn, staring her down. "She needs to accept that the Tony Gitano portion of her life is over now and move on before she gets herself whacked."

"You've got no idea what the hell I need!" The staring match left a space between them and Kimiko, a way out. "Way to talk, like I'm not here." I darted through before the Tanuki could stop me. But I felt a warm tingle somewhere near my elbow, which told me she'd tried, anyway.

I turned the corner, heading down to the other end of the hall and my room. I kept going past the elevator and looked back over my shoulder to see if any of them had followed. As I saw that they'd stayed put breath poured from my mouth, cooling the tears on my cheeks.

That' was when I bumped something flat and papery and ended up falling and whacking my head on the hardwood. A rustle and a slap met my ears, along with a little dismayed noise, vaguely familiar. I blinked, lifting my arm in an entirely useless attempt to get up. I saw a head of long, straight hair a paler platinum than my own.

"Are you okay, Miss Adler?" Sir Albert Dunstable, Sidhe knight of the queen's court, tossed his head, peering at me over the wire rims of the glasses he didn't need in the Under.

"Hoo, boy." I sighed. "I think so." A glance at the floor confirmed my suspicions. I'd knocked a pile of papers out of his arms, scattering them all over the floor in front of my room. "Sorry about your file."

"Your file, actually." Albert let go of my hand, then reached over to scoop stray paper into the manila folder still in the crook of one arm. "I brought everything Mr. Ichiro wanted you to look over before we're in session this evening. Are you sure you're all right?"

"I bumped my head and my dignity, that's all." I shuffled some of the fallen documents into an untidy pile, realizing that many of them were photos.

"Are you sure?" He opened the folder and put it on the floor to make for easier cleanup. "You look, um, unwell." His stack of papers went into the folder.

"More like unkempt. I woke up too early." I put my collection on top of his. "You can tell Mr. Ichiro that this won't affect the trial."

"No, that's not what I'm talking about, Miss Adler." He closed the folder, then picked it up. After that, he offered me a hand up.

"Then I don't get what you mean." I shook my head and stood on my own, mostly to see if I could do it myself. My head felt like a soft-boiled egg. "And call me 'Olivia,' please."

"Then call me Al. And listen, Olivia." Albert leaned against the wall while I unlocked the door to my room. "I overheard those three in the hall, what they said at you."

"That's absolutely none of your business." I pushed the door open and stepped across the threshold into my room, standing to block him from entering. Albert was Seelie and Gee Nome Unseelie. They'd have trouble occupying the same room on a good day, and I had the feeling this wasn't one of those.

"It's not. But Beth's wrong." Albert pushed his glasses up his nose. "You need to let yourself grieve, or mope as she put it. And you shouldn't give up on him."

"But Al, I've finally decided to accept the fact that Tony's—"

"Don't you dare." Albert stood with a posture that made me imagine him in a suit of armor. "Do not use that word next to Tony Gitano's name."

"Give me one reason." I stood there, unblinking.

"Hope, Olivia." He tucked his chin, eyes forward as though about to go to battle. Maybe he was after a fashion. "You need to keep on believing. For your own sake and everyone you care about."

"That makes no sense." I had to watch myself, be sure I didn't ask Al too many questions, or I'd owe him a favor.

"You've never been to the Under."

"I don't get what kind of point you're trying to make."

"It's not like this world." Albert shook his head. "The same rules don't apply. The Monarchs reign supreme, each in his or her own demesne. And the king has done something nearly unprecedented as far as you're concerned."

"Maybe I missed something because I'm all about the laws over here in the non-Faerie realm," I shook my head. "I don't get what's so odd about the Goblin King asking a favor from me."

"That wasn't some mere favor he called in." Albert tilted his head. "Didn't you realize that he set you on a Quest?"

"Wait." I froze in the doorway like an owl shifter statue. "He just wanted me to find some deadbeat and evict him or her from his demesne. That doesn't sound like a quest."

"Well, it is one. Of the search and retrieve variety."

"I guess you know what you're talking about. You've been one of the queen's knights for a couple of years now." Al took my blatant attempts to avoid asking him questions in stride.

"It's been three as a knight, after the year I spent as a page and the next as a Squire." Al sighed. "It feels like forever, though."

There was something I had to know, and the only way to find out was to ask at least one direct question. You only live once, right?

"If you don't mind my asking, are you happy?"

"That's a personal question."

"I'm sorry. It's personal because it's so general and specific at the same time." I took a deep breath and started again. "What I really mean is, I'm worried about how much of a chore Quests generally are and want to know whether it's possible to be happy doing them."

"They are, and they aren't." Al's eyes got as distant as the peak of Mount Everest. "My queen is demanding, exacting in her standards, and her rule is law. A harder sort of law than the mortal ones we've been preparing to practice here. The king is an entirely different kind of ruler."

"How so?" I stopped short of putting my hand over my mouth or kicking myself for being sloppy and asking a second question.

"I'm sure your Gnomish assistant can tell you more than I know, but I have heard rumors." He smirked.

"I don't mind listening to those." I raised an eyebrow.

"Mainly, they say that his rules bend. In fact, he expects flexibility." Al's smirk grew into a smile. "I've been given to understand that the more rules bent and boundaries pressed while on his Quests, the greater the reward."

"So, I can expect a longer and stranger trip than Ed's little adventure this spring?"

"Stranger, yes." He shrugged. "Longer is up for debate."

"And I've gone and asked you three questions like a total idiot." I hung my head, then shook it. I looked back up again and got a crick in my neck. "Ow."

"Don't worry. I can't demand a favor from you while you assist the king."

"I bet that's because I'll be on his side of the Under."

"Exactly. And don't worry too much about owing me. You were bound to owe me something simply because we are interning at the same firm."

"Interesting." I tilted my head AND The stupid crick in it twinged. "I wonder how much Mr. Ichiro owes your mother."

"Nothing at all. In fact, she's still paying off a twenty-three-year-old debt to him."

"Wow. I bet that's an interesting story." I would have nodded or otherwise physically indicated my curiosity but didn't want to aggravate my stupid neck.

"It is, and if I knew it, I'd tell it. All I can say is that it involved an aunt I've never met. You need to look at that file and make it to the courthouse by an hour after dusk."

"I'll see you then, Al. And thanks." I grabbed the door, preparing to close it.

"After ending up in my debt, I ought to be the one thanking you, Olivia. Good afternoon."

I watched him go, wondering why his straight back and

square shoulders gave the impression of some old and secret sadness. The file held photos of crime scenes, evidence, and a report to the Federal Bureau of Extrahuman Investigation. I had way too much to do in too little time. Beth had been right about one thing, the same thing Al had implied when he declined to tell the story of Mr. Ichiro and Mrs. Dunstable.

I didn't have time to dwell on the past.

CHAPTER FOUR

Olivia

The night court loomed ahead of me in the darkness, except it didn't look dark by that point. Going off the meds had enhanced my night vision. I stared at it, the tall, granite-gray lines of its Art Deco architecture making it more imposing than Batman in a dark alley. I wondered what it'd be like to shift and fly up to perch on the top like a gargoyle, but I'd fail this city if I didn't head inside and help Mr. Ichiro do his job to defend an innocent man.

My feet pattered on the stone steps, flat and without an echo. I pushed through the door, letting the bailiff wave a wand over me and the briefcase I carried even though I'd just passed through the rectangular metal detector around the door. The contraptions looked like wedding arches for robots, or maybe cyborgs. I closed my eyes and drew a deep breath, battling the image my mind conjured. It had me walking with my father down a long aisle lined with my friends and packmates, with Tony at the end.

"You okay, Miss?" The bailiff's forehead was a concerned crinkle.

"Yeah, fine."

"Sure, whatever." A hand clapped me once on the shoulder. "I've got it from here, George."

I glanced right to find Josh Dennison, the wolf-shifter Alpha of Tinfoil Hat, wearing a security badge. It made sense. He was majoring in Extrahuman Criminal Justice and was expected to join the Providence Police Force's Extrahuman Unit after graduation. He held out one hand, gesturing toward the hallway that led to the courtroom. "Hey, I want to apologize for Beth. She was way out of line."

"No, she wasn't." I looked down, watching the inlaid marble pass under my feet as I stepped along. "Beth's had an experience I wouldn't wish on anyone."

"It doesn't excuse her for making assumptions about your life, though." Josh snorted. "Beth's temper came back from the dead with Ren. It's good for some reasons, but not so much in the socialization department."

"It's all good, Josh." I stopped to wait by the closed courtroom door.

"Okay." He turned to face me. "Now, what's this I hear about the Goblin King?"

"Oh, he wants me to help him find some kind of interloper in his demesne."

"Did he say who?" Josh scratched his chin. I wondered whether he was thinking about his brother, Derek, who'd gone missing seven years before. But he'd been hauled off for shifting in public by some Psychic Federal agent named Natalie Johnson, not Unseelie faeries. His family hadn't been able to find out where he'd been incarcerated, either. I knew because I'd read the report.

"No." I shook my head. "He only said it's someone who doesn't belong there."

"Huh." Josh sighed, then stopped scratching his chin to run one hand through his hair. "Well, you should drop by Nox's place when you get a chance. She'd been on that side of the Under before and might have some useful intel for you."

"Um, but…" I wasn't sure I wanted to correct my Alpha, but he never seemed to mind much when Lynn or Blaine did, so I went ahead. "Well, won't I just be an owl the whole time I'm there, anyway?"

"Oh, right. Yeah." He put his hands on his hips. "Hmm. I wonder why the king wants you there, then. It's not like you could talk to this person if you find them. Or fight them, even. Unless it's a mouse shifter or something." Josh chuckled. "Someone like that would be terrified of your owl."

"I mentioned that to Ron…um, I mean the king, but he said he wanted me specifically."

"Leaping Luna!"

"What?"

"Did you just—" Josh blinked. "I mean, the Goblin freaking King had you call him by one of his borrowed given names!"

"Shh." I glanced around, but the hall was still empty. Mostly. There were a few ghosts in there, but they hadn't so much as looked at us. "It's not something I want the world to know about, okay?"

"Okay. But wow. That's serious." Josh narrowed his eyes. "When was the last time a Magus checked your coincidence? Have you had a Psychic reading recently?"

"I dunno." I shook my head. "Well, Mr. Ichiro checked my Luck last night, but I don't have time for any of that." I jerked a thumb at the massive oak door, which had started to creak open.

"Yeah. Okay, right on." Josh nodded. "I mean it about going to see Nox. You never know what information might come in handy."

"Okay, I'll do that." Mentioning that I didn't have time seemed like a bad idea. I turned to look at the courtroom entrance, watching a flicker of dim light grow between the two wooden panels of the double doors.

Josh waved, glancing back over his shoulder as he walked away. The wolf shifter probably thought the doors opened by telekinesis or all on their own. But some ghosts in uniform pulled it open even though owl shifters like me weren't supposed to be able to see them. I gave each of them a nod, then headed inside.

I'd been in the night court building before, but never the big courtroom. The place reminded me of a cave if only caves had Rococo carvings at the bases of their walls. Columns that tapered toward the middle like conjoined stalactites and stalagmites framed the Judicial bench, also ornately carved. I wondered how, before the reveal, anyone could have believed this room was mundane. The sense of wonder it inspired was like the first night I remembered seeing the full moon.

Setting the briefcase down, I sat in the first row. Unzipped, the case reminded me of some reptilian creature who'd choked on a ream of paper. It didn't take long to sift through to find the photos and documents we'd need and set those aside.

There was still time, so I flipped open the report to the Federal Bureau of Extrahumans. My eyes bugged out at all the dropped names. I'd expected to see Brodsky, Watkins, and Thurston mentioned, but Hertha Harcourt? Gino Gitano was there, and Tony's name sat at the bottom of the potential contacts list, right under Detectives Weaver and Klein of the Newport PD.

Closing my eyes, I thought back to Kimiko's story about Spring Break in Newport. Tony had played informant for a drive-by shooting with Blaine Harcourt as its target. His stepfather Wilfred had also died that week, and the circumstances surrounding his death were baffling. I checked the notes and found a few lines about him. Pharaoh's Rats in the Harcourt hoard? No wonder they'd dinged the FBE.

That'd be a second crime against extrahumanity, if intentional. Introducing predatory magical critters into a non-native habitat was just a misdemeanor, but planting them in a dragon's home is a flat-out felony of the premeditated murder variety. If the feds knew back in the spring, why hadn't they been involved since then? I leaned back in the chair, trying to think of some reason. The only thing that made sense to me was that they'd sent an agent who'd failed.

"Miss Adler." Mr. Ichiro set his epic briefcase down on the defendant's table. "Thank you for coming prepared. However, you've taken the incorrect seat."

"Oops." I got up, managing not to spill everything off my lap. Then I headed to the other side of the table, set the documents down in a neat pile in front of me, and tucked the FBE file away.

A few minutes later, a bailiff escorted Pavlo Brodsky in from the secure entrance and ushered him to the vacant seat beside Mr. Ichiro. I hadn't actually seen him since before he got arrested, only heard his voice on the recordings I'd transcribed.

"I see you got the suit," said Mr. Ichiro.

"Da." Professor Brodsky cleared his throat. "I mean, yes. Thank you." He brushed a speck of lint off his sleeve. "Are you sure about this brown?"

"Yes." Mr. Ichiro nodded. "It gives an academic impression, which is what we want on the day your colleague testifies."

"I can hardly believe he recovered in time." Professor Brodsky shook his head. "It's miraculous."

Professor Brodsky couldn't hear the faint squeak of rubber wheels on the stone floor. Mr. Ichiro's faint grin hinted that his hearing was on a par with my own. I turned halfway around in my seat to see Nathaniel Watkins in his wheelchair, Josh pushing him along. More guests, witnesses, and the prosecution team filed in after them.

"Miraculous me has some ghosts, a medium, and Adler here to thank." Professor Watkins chuckled. "Hello, Pavlo."

"You look like death, Nate."

"I know." Professor Watkins chuckled again. "It was all the rage back during the Emo craze, but I seem to have missed that trend."

"How can you joke when the one who did this to us is still out there?" Professor Brodsky paled. He refrained from looking in the jury box's direction. I would have too, were I in his shoes.

"How can you not?" Watkins winked. I couldn't help but giggle a little. "See? Adler gets it. Keep that sense of humor. You'll need it."

A door closed on one side of the bench and I automatically stood, even before the bailiff gave the announcement to rise for the right honorable Judge Beatrice Fiori. I glanced at the prosecution's table just in time to see Karen Gunn, the Assistant District Attorney, tuck something black and shiny into the briefcase in front of her.

Since it was the second night of the *State of Rhode Island versus Pavlo Brodsky*, the lawyers had already given their opening statements. Karen Gunn presented evidence analysis of two dead vampires' remains, along with photos and video of the destruction at the Nocturnal Lounge, PPC Library, and Henry's apartment building. An MCSI had gone on the stand to explain the magic and Psychic powers needed to make such attacks with wards in place. Justice Fiori called the court to order, and Karen Gunn rose to call her third witness.

"The prosecution calls Henry Baxter to the witness stand." The pointy leather toe of Karen's shoe tapped in counterpoint to the stamp of Henry's Doc Martins.

Henry wore a shirt, tie, and sports coat instead of his Sisters of Mercy t-shirt and the leather jacket with the painted Bauhaus logo. The Alliance Medallion that officially linked the vampire to a shifter pack dangled from his tie clip. He stepped up to the stand, then followed the swearing-in process. They gave vampires the option to swear on something other than the Bible,

39

but Henry didn't request that option. His hand looked right at home on the pebbled black leather binding of the book.

Karen Gunn paced toward the witness stand, stopping less than a foot from the court reporter, who looked like he wasn't happy about the invasion of personal space. The prosecutor tapped her foot three more times on the floor, her sleek ponytail bobbing along like a chestnut- and gray-streaked robin, the red blouse under her gray jacket only enhancing that impression.

"Mr. Baxter, how many times were you attacked last January?"

"Three."

"And you say two different creatures came after you, correct?"

"Yes, that's right."

"Name them for the court, please, Mr. Baxter."

"The first two times I got attacked by a Grim and the third time, it was a Spite."

"I see." Miss Gunn turned her back on the stand and Henry, facing the Judge. "No further questions for this witness, Your Honor."

"That's no good." Professor Brodsky stared down at the table in front of him. I understood what he meant. Brodsky was the only Summoner in the Rhode Island Registry to control both a Grim and a Spite. Mr. Ichiro wouldn't be able to ask about anything besides the attacks or the creatures on cross-examination. All the same, my boss got up and strode across the stone floor to smile up at Henry.

"Mr. Baxter, what else did you see during those attacks?"

"Objection." Karen stared daggers at Yoshi Ichiro. "Indefinite question, Your Honor."

"Sustained, Miss Gunn." Judge Fiori nodded. "Narrow your focus, Mr. Ichiro."

"Please name any other humans or extrahumans present at the start of each attack, Mr. Baxter."

"The first time, I was with Tony Gitano, cat shifter." Henry sighed. "No one else was there. The second time, I was with

Maddie May, Umbral magus. And the third time, this was the Spite attack, again with Miss May."

"Thank you, Mr. Baxter." Mr. Ichiro bowed his head to Judge Fiori. "No further questions, Your Honor."

Yoshi paced back to our table, grinning at Karen as they passed each other. He took his seat, and she waited for Henry to vacate the witness stand. "I call my next witness, Margot Malone."

I glanced at Mr. Ichiro. We hadn't anticipated the prosecution calling an extrahuman expert witness to the stand.

"Miss Malone, you're a Summoner, like the defendant, correct?"

"Yes." Margot's coppery curls bounced on her shoulders as she nodded.

"Exactly how long have you been summoning supernatural and pure faerie creatures?"

"Since nineteen sixty."

Karen Gunn took five clicking steps over to the prosecution's table and pressed a button on her briefcase. A magigraphic display hovered in mid-air. "I'd like you to look at these photos taken by MCSI at the defendant's apartment. What are the items in the display, Miss Malone?" Karen stepped toward Margot again.

"These objects are anchors creatures have an affinity to. Summoner-class Psychics like me can use them to call for aid."

"Can anchors call dangerous hunting hounds like the Umbral Grim and the Seelie Spite that tortured and killed two vampires and attacked Mr. Baxter?"

"Yes, if the Summoner has an agreement with a Grim or a Spite, they can make an anchor together."

"How long does it take to develop powers strong enough to get an agreement with either of the creatures you mentioned?" Karen clicked back toward the briefcase again.

"Half a century of study, at least."

"This is a record of Professor Brodsky's credentials from Providence Paranormal College faculty archives." Karen pressed the button again, and the display showed a doctoral diploma inked in Russian. The display captioned the image with an English translation, naming the institution as the Minsk Psychic Institute. "Please tell me how many years of study it takes to get this degree and read the date, Miss Malone."

"A Ph.D. takes from twelve to fifteen years of study at a college like PPC from Baccalaureate all the way up. And that date says January twentieth, nineteen forty."

"No further questions, Your Honor." Karen sat down on the edge of her seat.

"Miss Malone," Mr. Ichiro stood, then pressed his own button for our magigraphic display. The image went back to the evidence photo. "Please point out the Grim and Spite anchors in this picture."

"Um, I'm sorry. I can't." Margot shook her head. "None of the items in the photo anchor those particular creatures."

I heard the faint creak of wood under duress, then turned my head to see Karen Gunn's hands gripping the edge of the prosecution's table, knuckles white as bleached bone.

"For the record, please state your level of Summoner education, Miss Malone."

"Oh. I'm a doctoral candidate with just about a year left to go, Mr. Ichiro."

"When did you become a doctoral candidate?"

"Objection, irrelevant."

"Overruled," Judge Fiori said. "Credentials of an expert witness are relevant, Miss Gunn. The answer, Miss Malone?"

"Nineteen sixty-eight, Your Honor."

"What's taken you so long?"

"Vampires weren't allowed at PPC until Headmistress Thurston took over. When I got turned, the school suspended my candidacy."

"No further questions, Your Honor." Mr. Ichiro bowed his head to Margot, then turned to take his place at our table again.

"Redirect." The left corner of Karen Gunn's mouth pulled into a smirk that could have beaten one of Blaine Harcourt's for cockiness by a country mile. "Miss Malone, you were one of the defendant's students before you got turned. Did he have anchors for Grims and Spites during that time?"

"Yes."

"No further questions, Your Honor." Karen stayed in her seat but turned her head to look at the person sitting behind me. She smiled. "The Prosecution calls Professor Nathaniel Watkins to the stand."

I stood up to help, but Josh got there before me. He wheeled the professor's chair toward the witness stand, where he offered help, but Nate Watkins shook his head and took a few shuffling steps before being seated. They swore him in, and Miss Gunn wasted no time.

"When did you first meet Pavlo Brodsky, Professor?" The prosecutor clicked toward the witness stand, stopping next to that poor court reporter again.

"My father sponsored him when he immigrated from Russia in 1944."

"So, you were a baby."

"Yes." Professor Watkins nodded. "I don't remember a time when I haven't known my colleague."

"What's your opinion of the defendant, Professor?" Miss Gunn smiled.

"He's a pretentious jerk." Professor Watkins gave Brodsky a smile as sour as vinegar. "Some of his research topics are outdated and insensitive."

"Inhumane, then?"

"No." Professor Watkins shook his head. "I said 'insensitive.'"

"So, the defendant has engaged in such behavior?"

"Oh, all the time." Professor Watkins grinned. "Miss Malone

does it too. Ordering wild creatures around is generally insensitive, in my opinion."

"Have you ever witnessed Pavlo Brodsky behave inappropriately toward people, human or otherwise?"

"He's behaved inappropriately toward me, yeah." The professor's lips twisted into a smirk. "He tried to ground me instead of leaving that to my parents."

"Tell me about the incident between you and your colleague on the day Headmistress Thurston announced the new open admissions policy at the college."

"Oh, we nearly came to blows over the fact that vampires were allowed."

"Explain." Karen Gunn smiled like she'd just gotten a royal flush in a high-stakes poker game.

"I thought it was a great idea. Brodsky didn't. Mostly he worried that campus wouldn't be safe with vampires allowed to live and study there." Professor Watkins stroked his goatee. "And he was right. The campus isn't safe."

"I thought you said you disagreed." That poker victory smile froze like a deer in the headlights.

"I did and still do, but for a different reason." The professor gazed at the prosecutor exactly like she was one of his students about to utter an incorrect answer. "Vampires and shifters and faeries should be at PPC because it's desire and hard work that make a great student, not their diet or shape. But the campus isn't safe, and it's not the students at fault. It's the people objecting to them."

"No further questions." Karen glared like a Gorgon at Mr. Ichiro as she headed back to her table. He sat like a serene gadfly on the surface of a pond until she was seated.

"Professor Watkins." Mr. Ichiro rose and faced the man in the witness stand. "Tell me about last fall, when my client asked for your help."

"Brodsky came into my office looking like a train wreck and

told me he couldn't sleep. He'd been having nightmares again, same as right after he immigrated here." Professor Watkins sighed. "I asked him if he was back in therapy again since that helped him before. He said he was, also that he'd tried Sominex and Ambien, and a few stronger pills, too. But he wanted me to help him find something magipsychic even though such devices are highly regulated."

"And did you help him?"

"I tried to. I called a Psychic friend, but it went nowhere. The last time I asked Pavlo about the sleep troubles was right before exams last year. He said he'd found a solution on his own, and it was taken care of." Professor Watkins smirked.

A pencil clattered to the marble floor under the prosecutor's table. Professor Brodsky leaned back in his chair, shoulders finally positioned at a level approaching normal.

"Thank you, Professor Watkins." Mr. Ichiro bowed his head to Judge Fiori. "No further questions, Your Honor."

A shuffle, rustle and click sounded to my right as Karen Gunn closed her briefcase. Two bright red splotches high on her cheekbones were the only color left on her face. Her eyes glittered like bullet casings on cracked pavement.

"The State rests, Your Honor."

We took a recess. Professor Watkins stuck around, which I hadn't expected, given his condition. If it were me stuck out of my body for five months and change, I'd have wanted to curl up under a blanket with a good book for a year and a day.

During the recess, it was my turn to help. I had to manage the pictures I'd looked over and feed them into the device connected to the magipsychic display. After court had convened again, Mr. Ichiro presented evidence while I brought each piece into view for the court on the display.

The contents of Pavlo Brodsky's medicine cabinet, photos of his bedroom and home office, and his laboratory at PPC all took a turn on the magipsychic equivalent of an overhead projector. The final display was a report from the Extrahuman Registry.

Brodsky's official record designated him as a Summoner and listed every creature he could summon. The Grim was there, as was the Spite. The last page of the Registry's record contained a Psychiatric evaluation, but most of it was redacted. The parts we could read included diagnoses of Generalized Anxiety Disorder and Insomnia. This record showed the name of his most recent Psychiatrist and our list of witnesses for the next court session.

Judge Fiori adjourned the court for the evening. I gathered the file and handed it to Mr. Ichiro. The trial wasn't anywhere near over, but I had an agreement with a Faerie monarch to honor and had enough field experience to keep my internship. The sleepless half-day was catching up to me. I had to hope I could handle whatever the Under decided to throw at me.

As it turned out, the Faerie realm was the least of my troubles.

CHAPTER FIVE

Tony

I woke without dust and ash in my nose, wondering whether I was a ghost like Horace and company. Then, I started hacking up a lung as though I hadn't breathed in days. My body trembled like a soprano's voice above high C, probably a side effect of feeling like I'd been entombed in ice. I tried to get a grip but couldn't, and figured if I wasn't dead, I might soon be.

Something that felt like a silk-wrapped brand pressed against my forehead. I opened my mouth, voice straining, but I didn't scream. Not in the human sense, anyway. What came out sounded like the springtime catfights that always broke out behind the old house on Broad Street where I grew up.

"Hush now." The white-hot sensation at my brow toned down to a front-of-hearth warmth, then dissipated to settle the permafrost chill in my bones. "Be at peace while you still can, Godson."

I tried opening my eyes, but they balked like a team of spooked mules. I tried a few more times before they cracked open to let in light and sight, but after that, I had to blink because

I couldn't believe my stubborn old peepers. No extrahuman in his right mind would have if they'd woken from death and the first thing they saw was a Kitsune. I felt less like a cat of the shifter variety and more like one in a box, dead and alive at the same time, or maybe neither.

"You don't exist." My words creaked like the gate to a neglected graveyard. "Either that, or I really am sleeping with the fishes."

"Tch." The woman shook her head, red-brown curls bobbing around her heart-shaped face. "Feathered things are much better for sleeping with than fish, don't you agree?"

"So, am I dead like you?"

"I could take offense," the Kitsune said, "but I won't. Yes, these are real." She reached up to stroke one of her black-tipped pointed ears. She giggled as something moved to her left. "And these are real, too." I stared at the tails that shouldn't be attached to this woman. "Reality is amazing, and full of all kinds of surprises."

"Yup. You're definitely not just a regular fox shifter." I blinked a few more times. "They only get one tail and can't do the partial shifting thing."

"Your perspective guides your assumptions, of course. If only the king and all his courtiers could look at this situation as you do." She released a low chuckle.

"The Goblin King?" I looked at her face, noting the mirthful twinkle in her eyes. I squinted at the ears again, and the tails, willing my eyes to bring them out of focus the way you're supposed to when trying to see through a glamour. But this wasn't a glamour. The crazy lady actually did have tails, plural.

"Yes. Only one of the king's tithed subjects ever saw me for what I truly am. Please, ask me more questions. I love adding to my ledger in the credits column." Her smile was similar to a vampire's but the canines had thicker points. Her laugh barked like some know-it-all terrier, and I bet dollars to donuts her tongue would have lolled out if she'd been more amused. She'd just implied that the faerie rules about favors applied to her, too. I wasn't sure whether that was true because ancient accounts of Kitsunes differed. Fun.

"Kitsunes are extinct." I couldn't remember much more about the magical fox shifters than that. Being dead or whatever had probably scrambled my brain because I should have known better. I'd read something about how the tails worked but couldn't recall exactly what. I put the thought off like delaying Windows updates while finishing homework.

"Yes." The Kitsune shook her head. "And no." She nodded. "Kitsune are only just barely not extinct. We shouldn't be." She unwound a glimmering red scarf from the hand she'd held against my forehead, slipped something into her pocket, then draped the fabric over her ears. She looked more like a character on that TV show about the flying nun than a magic fox trying to hide her identity. "Honestly, what do they teach you at that school?"

"I've learned a lot, actually." I pressed my palms against the mossy earth, trying to sit up. It wasn't very effective. "And please, ask me more questions, nameless Kitsune…er, Lady. Yeah, you're dressed like a faerie lady. I'd bet you've visited the king a time or three."

"Ah!" She clapped her hands. "Yes, even if the lessons are inferior to what I'd teach, you've minded your studies both in and out of the classroom. My work in the Under is nearly done, though. And that's one of the many reasons I've decided to, hmm…" Her lips curved up. "Reconnect with my godson."

"But I was—" I shivered. "No, I couldn't have been dead."

"Oh, but you were." She barked a single sharp laugh. Her eyebrows tilted downward, drawing together as she narrowed her eyes. "And you don't remember? This is the eighth time you've suffered fatal injuries, you know."

"You're more annoyingly vague than that self-absorbed dragon-man, Blaine Harcourt."

"Oh, stop." The Kitsune held her sides and shook with laughter. "That's the funniest thing I've heard all decade! Dragon-like? And comparing me to a Harcourt, no less. Oh, that is literally rich!"

I wondered whether all Kitsunes had mood swings like this one seemed to. "Look, I'm not asking you any more questions, Lady Godmother Kitsune whatever, but unless you like being called 'hey you,' a name would be nice."

"Call me 'Kiki.'"

I breathed a sigh of relief at the fact she hadn't asked me to call her my Lady or even worse, some weird short form of godmother that might show her up as even more egotistical than Blaine. After that, I sucked in a breath that got caught in my chest when I tried to get up again. I hissed like gravity itself threatened my territory, then turned on my side. Something was wrong with me, and it wasn't only my being mostly or all dead for however long, either.

I stared across the moss past Kiki's slipper-clad feet. Past the line of trees I lay under, dark waves greeted a black sand beach. The ocean horizon stretched, full of tequila sunrise colors that didn't progress. In this place, time was a feature of the landscape. The breeze hummed and sang with magic I wasn't sure how I sensed. I stared at my perfectly normal human-shaped hands, then reached up to touch my face. I had whiskers and not the kind you get with five o'clock shadow, either.

Sighing, I ran that hand through my hair and stopped when it made contact with one pointy ear, as furred as Kiki's own. I sat finally, still reeling from the strongest bout of déjà vu I'd ever experienced. After that, I looked up. Kiki had just finished wrapping a black and gold shawl around her waist, covering her tails. My mind finally connected some dots.

Kitsunes were magical shifters. No one was sure whether they had inherent magic like dragons and Tanuki or used an enchanted item like Kelpies and Selkies. The accounts agreed on one thing, however. In the Under, they'd remain in a partially human form, although that didn't happen in the regular world unless they had to do a bit of magic—usually air and lightning—which combined to make the Foxfire they'd been known for. The more tails they had, the more power, with nine being the most one could carry.

I'd also read that Kitsune actually separated from the form they weren't using, leaving half of themselves behind in the Under whenever they weren't shifted. This extended their lifespans like faeries. I wasn't sure whether asking them questions worked the same way, but Kiki sure acted like it did.

Mundane shifters got stuck in their animal shapes in the Faerie realm. Bobby or Josh would have to go on all fours and limit their vocabulary to growls and barks here—except here I was, not sounding like a Meow Mix commercial or craving sardines. I sat contemplating my ears and whiskers, then reached behind me to check on my latest suspicion. Yup, I had a tail, too.

"I'm not in my cat form, Kiki." I stopped staring at the ocean and looked at her. "And I want to know why."

"You're awfully perceptive for a fellow who's spent most of the last week dead." She smirked and offered me a hand up, which I refused. "All you need is deductive reasoning to make a huge discovery. Or ask me another question, Antonio."

"Ugh." I wrinkled my nose at the name I never used. "It's Tony. And stop talking like a fortune cookie; I get it already. I'm some kind of magical shifter. Should have figured that out after I whipped out a glamour in the Grim attack at the Nocturnal Lounge." Glamour came naturally to me after that first reflexive usage. I still had no clue why or how, but I wasn't about to ask Kiki more questions if it'd put me in her debt, godmother or not.

"Now you begin to understand." She clapped her hands. "I love new discoveries."

"Must suck, then. Being stuck here for however long." I sat up on my own, considering she'd started using her hands to clap instead of help. Sitting, I could manage. Standing, probably not yet, even with help.

"That doesn't matter now. You're starting a whole new adventure." This time, Kiki rubbed her hands together like a dragon might have while gazing at a pile of gold.

"Thanks, Lady Obvious." I rolled my eyes, internally refusing to refer to her as "Captain." That rank was pretty high in the Under. A captaincy was two ranks past a lord or lady. It was right up there with knight, but it carried more authority at sea.

"The best thing about this particular beginning is, it's the end of something else." Kiki gave that barking laugh again. I hadn't decided whether I liked it yet, or her, for that matter. After all, I didn't have the best track record with parental figures.

"I hope you're talking about an end to my time here in the Under so I can go home." I wasn't about to tell her that going home would likely get me killed. Again.

"No. Today is the first day of the rest of your lives, Tony Gitano." My godmother smiled.

I wondered whether this Kitsune was actually my spiritual guardian or just pulling one over on me, but if she followed faerie rules, she couldn't flat-out lie about something that important. Neither monarch could abide lying about family.

"I bet you don't even know what a fortune cookie is, Kiki." I flicked my tail in her general direction.

"As a matter of fact, I do." She licked her chops. "So much crunch, and they taste like cyanide smells. I love them so."

"Great." I lowered my head, face-palming with both hands. Kiki the Kitsune was nuttier than the almonds in those cookies. Morbid, too. But whether that was cat lady or serial killer kooky, I couldn't tell. Either way, I wasn't comfortable being alone with her anymore.

"There's got to be someone else around who can help me." I

lifted my head, then turned to face the dark side of the demesne. "Gee! Gee Nome! That little twit's got to be around here somewhere." I put my hands on either side of my mouth and called a third time for the friend of my undead friend. Hey, I'm a Rhode Islander. I know a Gnome. "Gee!"

"The Gnome can't hear you, which is a good thing." Her ears flattened for a moment, marring the wimple effect they made under the scarf. "We're not ready to meet all the king's men, and all of his horses are even worse." She had a point. Kelpies were seriously scary business.

"Look, we're in the Under and could use more help. And I ain't going to the queen's people." I crossed my arms and pouted, laying on the surliness thicker than cream cheese on a bagel.

"Why not?" She sounded genuinely curious, as though she played both sides and expected me to do the same, or something. But I wasn't messing around, not when she'd left an opening like that.

"Oh!" I pointed, bouncing with glee. "That's a question! We're even-steven now, Kiki!"

"Yes. One question. And you must answer it." My godmother raised an eyebrow, somehow doing the intimidating mother thing better than my pal Fred's Italian mama.

"Fine. The queen's allied with this Extramagus, who's been working with my dad since Spring Solstice. They're like the League of Doom on steroids. I know two Seelie knights and a couple of Summoners, but I won't call them. They might be under oath to rat me out even if they don't want to. Right now, Dad's down some muscle, out one safe-house, and more vulnerable than he's been since I can remember. He thinks I'm dead. I could go to the Police, and he'd never see it coming. But I need out of the Under. And no offense, Kiki, but you don't seem like you'll be much help in that department."

The wind picked up, then it bench-pressed a half-ton. The air hummed and crackled with magic energy, with my godmother at

D.R. PERRY

the eye of that particular storm. She was about to call down lightning or a cyclone, or maybe both. Kiki towered over me, scarf
billowing in the gale. Her tails waved beneath the fabric. Oh,
yeah, with those, she was definitely powerful enough to make
fried cat-man out of me.

"Not much help?" Kiki's nostrils flared and her face length-
ened, growing decidedly more foxlike. Her hand went to a round
pouch hidden under the strongest glamour I'd ever seen. "Not
much help? I'll show you what help truly is, youngling!"

"Um, yeah. About that." I smirked at the angry Kitsune. If she
wanted to play faerie favor games, I'd go along. "You sort of owe
me now."

The static raising my hair vanished, and the wind gentled. A
chuckle floated along it—hers.

"Outfoxed." Kiki let go of the oval hilt, and it vanished again.
She smiled. "By a cat asking to be let out, no less. And that's as it
should be, considering what and who you are. You're uncannily
like your mother when you gloat, but of course, you never got a
chance to see her the way I did. Instead, you got that mustache-
twirler you call a father."

I'd put up with the danger of debt, my godmother's volatility,
and even the cheesy puns. My aim in this wasn't just about
getting out of the Under and putting dear old Dad behind bars
where he belonged; there was more at stake. My friends, my
school, the state of extrahuman affairs in all of Rhode Island. The
biggest pictures were always the easiest for me to see.

All the same, I'd do just about anything to learn more about
my mother, and Lady Kiki knew it. I couldn't ask about her,
though. I had one request from a powerful and possibly unique
creature. My friends back at school were up a creek, and I had to
choose a battle. Even a Kitsune with all nine tails couldn't go toe-
to-toe with an Extramagus, but she'd confound the kitty litter
out of my father. Knocking down one of Hopewell's allies took
priority over hearing her reminisce.

"Now, since I outfoxed you," I said, selecting my words as specifically as possible, "I need help eliminating my father from the entire extrahuman equation. You're an ancient Kitsune who said you'd show me what help is, so make with the showing already."

"We have to get something first." She held her hand down to me again, and this time, I let her help me to my feet. "Trust me, getting these items is essential to your success on both counts."

"Okay, so let's get the thingamabobs."

"Great Goblin King's Garters." Kiki smiled.

"Um, that's something a seriously scary Kelpie likes to say when everything's about to go sideways." I glanced up, down, and to either side of my godmother, looking for an ambush but Nox Phillips wasn't there.

"They're also exactly what we're looking for." She dropped a wink.

"I really didn't need the mental image of the Goblin King wearing a garter belt, Kiki. Maybe we can pick up some mind bleach while we go and get the unmentionables."

"The Goblin King's Garters are not costuming for the Rocky Horror Picture Show, Tony." She turned her head to the side, nose in the air, then waited, peering at me from the corner of her eye. I understood the dare and danger. She wanted more questions out of me.

"I'm not asking you how you've seen an old cult movie or what those garters actually are, so don't hold your breath." I flicked my tail, then tried to still it. Stupid thing was messing with my poker face.

"You're no fun." She shook her head, then headed off deeper into the forest. "I'm not the right audience for you to inspire breathlessness in anyway. The Garters were made by the king ages ago, at the start of the rift between Seelie and Unseelie. The queen recruited forces in her cause to impose order on the mortal realm. Roman lion shifters are not part of either court but at that time, they sided with the queen, so, he gave away his magical bow and its string to be wielded by the right person at the right time. It transmutes any arrow to a given creature's direst bane, Tony. One of his champions defeated three legions of lions by herself."

I ducked under branches and stepped over ferns, trying to keep up. "So what you're saying is, you want me to shoot my dad?"

"Hee!" Kiki continued in a sing-song voice. "You asked a question!"

The ancient and powerful Kitsune probably belonged in a kindergarten. I sighed, thinking of how, if I wanted to feel like a super-villain in the making, I'd have binge-watched *Dr. Horrible's Sing-A-Long Blog*.

"What's a ding-a-long-bong?"

"Sorry, my inside voice must have malfunctioned." I chuckled. "And you just asked a question too. So there."

"You kids today use too many pop-culture references." She waved a hand, and the underbrush parted. "You've got a lot to learn about being timeless, Antonio."

"You old fogeys use too many tired tropes."

"They're traditions, young one." It was Kiki's turn to sigh. "I'll admit they're awful most of the time, so let me have my moments when my ancient knowledge is useful."

"Horrible." I couldn't help it. I chuckled.

"Whatever." She waved one hand like we were on a float in a parade instead of hacking through the underbrush.

"I bet this is a longer trek than the one where they took the hobbits to Isengard." I spluttered as a clump of damp leaves hit me in the face.

"I actually get that one. And no, it's not long." Kiki stopped and turned around. "As a matter of fact, we're here."

I looked around, literally. We'd come to a nearly perfectly circular clearing in the woods. I could feel a clash of magical energies in the air as though this place existed at the border between the monarchical demesnes. Instead of dipping down into a hollow like most did outside the Under, the ground inclined. A faerie ring of toadstools squatted in a circle at the center, crowning a bare earthen mound.

"It's a Gnomehill." I scratched my head. "It's weird to look for a king's treasure in a place like this."

"Correct, and also not." Kiki smiled, making a gesture right out of a game show hostess's repertoire.

"I ain't barging in on some Gnome clan's house and tossing the place." I crossed my arms over my chest in the universal gesture for "humph."

"Don't worry, the Gnome whose home this is, we'll leave alone."

"I ain't saying that five times fast." I shook my head.

"It might be more useful to focus on the things you will do rather than what you will not." Kiki shrugged. "It helps when it's time to move forward instead of looking back."

"Maybe from your point of view." I sighed. "But I can't help remembering where I came from. It's like keeping one of those souvenirs that says, 'I survived a Mafioso parent and all I got was this lousy t-shirt,' if you catch my meaning."

"Perhaps it will be your greatest strength as well as your most glaring weakness." Kiki gestured at the Gnomehill. "But now, it's time to go in."

"I don't see any doors, or even a window." I stepped into the clearing to take a closer look. "Yeah, nope. Can't break and enter without an entrance."

"You'll have to make one with magic, of course." My godmother put her hands on her hips.

"But all I can do is throw and tear down glamour." I rolled my eyes. "I'm a pretty sorry excuse for a magical shifter."

"You're wrong." She raised that eyebrow again. "You're no Gamayun, but you pack a powerful magical punch. Just wing it."

"You say this like I'm an—" I shut my trap, choking down what I'd been about to say. Dad wasn't the only one who'd think I was dead. I'd been the flakiest friend in the universe, but there was one person in particular who could have been more than that, and she deserved better.

"Like you're an owl shifter." Kiki nodded, her expression grave instead of mocking or even ignorantly mirthful. "I know all about your bird friend. She's something special. But I forget her name."

"Olivia." Her name rolled off my tongue like honey from a spoon. I wished I could swallow it and hold on. Something changed in the energy of the surrounding air when I said her name. I wondered what that meant in the Under. I wondered how a Kitsune trapped here for centuries could know an owl shifter from New Jersey.

"Well, that's two for two." The Kitsune sighed. "Exactly like your mother again, Tony."

"She loved someone she couldn't be with, I guess." I blinked. I hadn't meant to use the L-word, even though it was true. The perspective I'd gotten from dying made that sort of thing crystal-clear.

"Yes." Kiki closed her eyes. "Celestina went against all sorts of good advice for his sake, too. She let her love and her visions guide her instead of common sense, much like one of her best friends."

"If Mom loved Dad so much, doesn't make much sense for him to have killed her." I couldn't let myself believe in love, no matter how much I might want to. Coincidence and mates, sure. That was desire, I thought. I was an idiot. "Love must be the most dangerous business in the known universe."

"You make many assumptions I don't have time to correct." Kiki opened her eyes, narrowing them at me. "Now, make with the magic already."

"Not sure why you can't do this since you've got plenty of

magic." I stepped out from under the trees and Kiki's scowl, stopping halfway up the hill. I didn't dare step on the faerie ring. They were supposed to be nastier than any ward on Gatto Gang territory, and I'd just gotten over one of those exploding in my face. Had Kiki really said I'd died eight times already? Maybe I actually remembered some of those times without realizing it. I'd walked away from a fair number of "accidents" I shouldn't have.

My questions and assumptions added up to one big heap of trouble if I didn't get answers in the future, but the Kitsune was right—I had no time to do anything about it in the present. I pointed a finger at the Gnomehill and tried to focus all my attention on it.

"Open Sesame!" Nothing happened. I dropped my arm and shook it, then spied a stick on the ground. Advanced Magical Theory students worked with wands, so why shouldn't I? Picking it up, I pointed it instead of one silly finger and tried something different.

"*Avada Kedavera!*" Nothing happened. I didn't count Kiki laughing as anything important. She knew Harry Potter but not Dr. Horrible. Lamest Kitsune ever. At least she'd heard of *Lord of the Rings*, and that gave me an idea. I didn't bother pointing this time. The idea had sparked some kind of vaguely familiar energy, sending it traveling from my head to spiral all the way down my body like a coil. Feeling a connection to the Under's earth, I spoke Gandalf's greeting from outside the gates of Moria.

"*Mellon!*"

Something rumbled under my feet, sounding like the hungriest giant in the known universe.

"Run, Tony!"

I didn't even get a chance to lift a foot before the sod and earth gave way under me, dumping me into a half-light as eerie as the inferno I'd endured back at the house in Olneyville. The mental crutch that had gotten me through a long line of dangerous situations was still in my head, so I leaned on it and counted.

"One hippopotamus, two hippopotamus, three hippopotamus, four hippopotamus, five—"

I hit dirt, or a light coating of it anyway, as I discovered when scuffing my toes against it. I closed my eyes, calling up the low-light vision that came with my cat-shifter abilities. When I opened them again, I shuddered.

"Tony! Make a noise if you're alive in there!"

"Gimme a hand up." I reached toward the hole.

Something blotted out the light from over my head, then Kiki hit the floor. She'd landed on her backside, too, not her feet like I had.

"Heh." I smirked. "Dog people."

"Fox people." She stood up, adjusting the sash that tried to hide her tails. "Get it right or pay the price."

"Foxes are canines." I shrugged.

"Kitsunes are magical. So are Kel...well, that information will cost you." She grinned.

"I'm dead-broke." I chuckled at my own joke. "Anyway, it seems kind of short-sighted to jump into an unknown hole instead of helping an ally out of one."

"Godson." Kiki brushed the dirt off her robe. "And it's not unknown to me. This is exactly where we want to be. Inside this particular Gnomehill."

"It doesn't look much like the kind of hole one of those talking potatoes would live in." I brushed dust off my coat.

"That's because this place hasn't always belonged to ornery pure faeries who wanted a hidey-hole." Kiki adjusted the scarf covering her ears. "Anyway, the Gnomes who live in here are some of His Majesty's most loyal subjects. They just have some strange ways of showing it, is all. I see they've at least kept the place secret, if not as tidy as its original owners would have liked."

"I'm not going to ask you who it belongs to or why they abandoned it." I peered down a long passage to my left. A faint tingle of energy prickled my skin when I considered heading in that direction, so I did. "I just hope it's not some kind of tomb or barrow."

"Don't worry," Kiki said. "It's got nothing to do with death."

"I bet you don't even know." I snorted.

"Well, I know about the Garters, and that they're here." She chuckled. "While I'm being honest, listen harder. I know more than I'm telling."

"I don't need reassurance, and I'll believe a magic bow is here when I—" I stopped just inside an open archway at the end of the passage, the sudden light piercing my eyes like glass shards. I had to rely on my other supernaturally sharpened senses.

The room smelled of long-dried roses, not something I'd expect to find in a Gnome's lair. Those little guys liked their trinkets sharp or shiny, usually both. Something as prim as a basket of potpourri or book of pressed flowers wasn't something they'd keep around.

After my eyes adjusted, I saw why this place didn't feel Gnomish. The chamber was a bedroom for regular-sized people. At one time, it might have been a cozy suite, combined with the stuff ancient faerie fertility rites used. The one thing I couldn't suss out was the vibe; whether the collection of items in here were geared toward getting with child or birthing one. At any rate, whatever energy the place had made all the hairs of my tail stand on end.

Woven tapestries and fabric hangings along stone walls had once made the space seem cozy and private. With all the dust, they just looked drab now. Magically lit braziers gave off light and warmth, flattering and warm enough respectively to make banishing modesty comfortable, but the specks of rust-red on the stone floors were definitely not from rose petals. The bed at the center was hip-height, at least for me. The place tried to push something to the surface of my mind but whatever it was got stuck like a stubborn hairball. My trench coat's collar felt too constricting all of a sudden, and I felt the urge to cut and run.

"You said the Goblin King's Garters had nothing to do with death or lingerie, but you bring me to a creepy bedroom." I put my hands on my hips and glared at my godmother. "Kiki, you've got a lot of 'splaining to do."

CHAPTER SIX

Tony

My godmother sighed. "We don't have time for that kind of explanation." For the first time, I got the idea that she might be tired of all the smoke and mirrors. Hinkiness, my packmates had called it. I was sick of it too, on more than one front.

"So, if the Garters are here, let's just get them and go already." I tapped my foot in the silence left behind by her refusal to explain further. I definitely wasn't asking her any more direct questions.

"I can't." Kiki shrugged her left shoulder, a gesture mirrored by dimpling in her right cheek. "I'm, umm, 'dog people' was how you put it. I can't even touch it."

"And I suppose I can because I'm cat people." I flicked the tip of my tail, finally angry for the first time since waking up in the thrice-cursed Under. I already hated the place, and I'd only been conscious there for maybe a half-hour. "Cat people are the ones this weapon was designed to destroy, so naturally, I've got to use the freaking thing. Yup. Makes perfect sense, just like every other rule in Faerie."

"That's an interesting sentiment from the fellow attending a magical college." Kiki leaned against one side of the arch. "A weapon's no good if there's a ban on it touching its targets. The Roman lions weren't the only cat shifters fighting in that war or the only neutral party to side with a monarch. A rogue cat shifter of the magical variety turned the weapon on them. Because they were magical, a few survived, but the big mortal wars of the twentieth century put an end to them. Now they're as extinct as Kitsunes. That's one reason the weapon's been hidden all this time, waiting for the right person to come along and use it as intended."

But a Kitsune stood in front of me, not extinct at all. Could she be the last of her kind? Did that mean there was just one of those rogue magical cat shifters left? Obviously, it was me. But what was I? And was I the last of a dying breed, or the first of a new one? These questions would have rocked a Watkins-led classroom, and possibly impressed Headmistress Thurston. They did nothing for me here, where I had to silence them or risk owing my life to Kiki. I set them aside.

"Yeah, well, that right person ain't me. I know diddly squat about archery. More likely to shoot my eye out than hit the bad guys." I rolled my eyes and shook my head. My problem was more that I didn't want to kill Dad, I only wanted justice of the legal variety. I wasn't about to tell a powerful and apparently bloodthirsty Kitsune that, however. "I'm not a fan of handling weapons that can kill me deader than the wise guys I'm worried about."

"Fan or not, it's what you'll need if you mean to face a shifter descended from the Roman lions of old." Kiki hedged her phrasing to avoid blatantly encouraging patricide, but the sentiment remained. She avoided looking me in the eye, too. No big surprise there.

I tried to shrug off the sense of wrongness that particular

word dragged into my mind after it. I owed Dad no loyalty. My father had tried to kill me. Succeeded, maybe even more than once. I swallowed bile and rage, wrinkling my nose. Still, I didn't want him dead, just out of the picture.

"Jail is best," I told myself. I'd never killed and didn't want to start, which Dad always gave as one reason I disappointed him. My brain clung to those three words and hammered them into a mantra. Could I follow it? I closed my eyes and prayed I'd never have to answer that question.

"Still doesn't do a thing about the fact that there aren't any magic weapons here. This room wasn't designed for fighters." I turned back to the suite, preparing to head back down the hall to see if I'd missed any other rooms. "It's for lovers. No faerie in their right mind would stash a magic weapon in such an oppositely purposed room. Glamour can only do so much when it comes to hiding something that doesn't belong somewhere."

"This place skirts all kinds of edges." Kiki's hand gripped my arm like a steel vise. "There's nothing in any of the king's rules that states exactly what kinds of battles make someone a fighter. You've got no idea what has happened in this room, and no right to judge. Go back in there and look harder."

"I won't find anything." I couldn't turn my head to meet her glare because it felt like a leaden weight. "And I already told you, I ain't got much magic."

"You found the entrance, so you'll find the Garters." She dropped her hand. "And technically, the weapon isn't meant for you to use, though you could brandish it in a pinch."

"That's what it sounds like when you say only I can touch it." I crossed my arms over my chest. "No point in looking for it if I ain't gonna bother using it."

"For a cat who easily dodges my attempts to trick questions out of him, you certainly are clueless." Kiki snorted. "I'll speak plainly just this once. Find the bow and its quiver of magic arrows. They are in this room. They will help your cause somehow."

"I wonder what kind of creature would use a weapon designed to kill feline shifters?" I turned back to examine the room and its contents more closely. "Someone like that has got to be terrifying."

"All the more reason for you to get the blasted thing. You want a frightful person in your debt, not holding a weapon without any obligation to you." My godmother put her hands on her hips, looking for all the world like she'd just told me I can't have any dessert if I don't eat my meat.

Before stepping into the chamber again, I glanced at Kiki. Maybe it shouldn't have bothered me to see the Kitsune stifling a laugh. I didn't give two shakes of my tail about how I should have felt. Most of my classmates would react to the news that Kitsune extinction had been highly exaggerated with the same enthusiasm I'd reserve for winning the lottery. They were a maddeningly optimistic bunch. Even the vampires barely brooded. But I knew better than the rest of them about too many things.

I'd watched the pack of them sympathizing together over consequences and the aftermath of shared experiences. It all started with the perfectly abnormal storm that had made Bobby want to hibernate and almost killed Lynn with a truck-ton of ice. A month ago, I'd started seeing ghosts. My whiskers had tingled with the prospect that we approached some bitter end, and I thought it'd be mine personally. I hadn't been wrong, either.

I stood at the foot of the bed, my head so far out of this "find the magic weapon game" it could have been on the *Enterprise*. Did my so-called packmates care about the loss of one little Omega kittycat? My dad had surely put on some fiasco of a memorial service to make himself look important, with a nice heaping side of innocent. I couldn't imagine anyone in Tinfoil Hat showing up except Olivia. Maybe Bianca, but probably just because she'd want to check for my ghost.

The only real friend I had in the pack was Fred Redford, and he couldn't have left the Under during his first tithed year without the queen's supervision. Then again, maybe she'd have gone. Yeah, that felt right somehow. The Extramagus, Richard Hopewell, was the closest thing to a friend a guy like my Dad could have. Hopewell had been angling for a gig as the queen's consort in exchange for tithing his badass self to the Seelie side of things. Dad would be all over cementing ties with that kind of power.

I shook my head, unable to concentrate on hunting for magic items like some sort of live-action *D&D* player. I took a stroll around the room instead, pacing its circumference and trying to acknowledge my negative thinking in hopes making like Queen Elsa and letting it go. Sure, everyone was hip-deep in Extramagus trouble. The rest of them had it easy. None came from a family with one parent murdered and the other an untrustworthy schemer. And then, I stopped with one foot in the air, feeling like the biggest *calabrese* moron in the known universe.

I was wrong. One of them did understand. Blaine Harcourt. He'd been too slow, missed his chance to stop an attack on his step-dad. Even his Luck-wielding mate couldn't help him. After that, Blaine had watched his literally venomous mother put the man who raised him out of his misery with a knife through the heart. I set my foot down and hung my head, ashamed of myself for going full judgmental on the dragon shifter. And that's when I saw the sickly green glow coming from under the bed.

The last thing I wanted to do was stick my hand into a space I couldn't see, looking for something made of copper. Silver killed werewolves. Iron killed faeries. Copper killed cat shifters. I dismissed the idea that I'd somehow be immune on account of my unexpected magical nature. No one was that lucky, not even the two Tanuki I knew.

But I had no choice. If Kiki was right, the only way to proceed against my father was to get the dang Garters. I wasn't going to grab blindly under the bed, though. I had a trick or three up my sleeve, literally. I always did.

I wasn't exactly sure when I realized I could activate magipsychic devices without help, but they were everywhere at my dad's safehouses and with his people. The Gatto Gang's main stream of illegal income was in "imports and exports" of black-market magically enhanced doodads. The crafters and buyers all thought shifters were great go-betweens since none of us could use the wares without an attunement done by a Magus or a Psychic. That was how things were supposed to work, but I was a monkey-wrench, and no one knew it.

The quartz lapel pin wasn't anything I'd ever wear in plain sight, but fixed to the lining of my trench coat, no one could see it. I pressed it between my bare arm and the floor, called on energy I shouldn't have been able to use, and activated it. After that, I eased my weight to my elbow and let the black fabric drape.

Light streamed from my open sleeve, illuminating the dusty space under the bed. A long, lean, shape swaddled in some kind of burlap fabric rested there, with a faint but telltale green glow coming from under and through a few threadbare spots in the fabric. I reached out with my lightless hand and grabbed what could only be a short bow and its quiver through the thickest section of burlap I could find. I pulled it toward me and out from under the bed. Then, I stood.

A question burned through my body like the time I'd accidentally-on-purpose gotten hit with a dart. Dad made me play a match against him after getting notice of my scholarship at PPC. I'd been sick, like my blood was on fire. I thought he'd poisoned me, but he couldn't have because I got better after a good fifteen hours of sleep. Maybe that was one of the deaths Kiki mentioned, and I'd come back without realizing it.

The bow thrummed through the fabric in my hand while the

glow under the burlap brightened. Could the magical weapon be reacting to my thoughts and feelings? How, though, if its purpose was killing people like me and was meant for someone else to use in the first place? Was I really that different from other cat shifters, or was this weapon more than what my godmother implied?

"You look like you've got questions," Kiki called from where she hovered over an urn by the doorway. "As much as I would absolutely love for you to ask them, we're out of time."

"Of course, we are." I strode back across the room toward her.

"Time waits for no cat or Kitsune." My godmother turned and led me back through the passage. She slipped the scarf off of her head and draped it around her neck, exposing her ears. After that, she twisted the scarf on her waist, revealing her tails. Were there more of them than I'd seen earlier?

I stopped when we got to the chamber we'd fallen into, wondering how in the name of magic we'd ever get out. Kiki just kept on walking toward the passage to the right, eight tails swishing behind her as she went. Yup, she had one additional tail, and I wasn't sure I wanted to know why. I followed her into a darkness even shifter eyes had trouble seeing through, lifting my arm so the light in my sleeve could lead the way. I'd seen this kind of darkness before and wanted no part of it ever again.

"Oh, no." I stopped. "We're not going through here."

"We will." Kiki kept walking. I had to press on or risk losing sight of her.

"But this is a Grim lair." I lowered my voice to a murmur, not even wanting to risk a whisper because the hissing might be too loud.

"I know." The Kitsune walked with steady, measured paces, lifting her feet with each step to avoid shuffling them.

"They're always hungry." I tried not to shudder but couldn't help myself.

"All the same, it's the only way out of here without wings or a Gnome." She twitched her ears, tilting them back toward me. "And we'd best do this quietly until we get out."

"Fine." I shut my trap, not because Kiki told me to, but because Grims were serious business.

I called on my glamour, cloaking us like I'd done back in January with Henry. It didn't work well against Grims in the Under, but it couldn't hurt. My godmother seemed alert, not afraid. I figured she must know something I didn't, either about the Grims or her abilities.

We went slow, almost maddeningly so. My jumpy nerves wanted me to just cut and run, but that would have been a bad idea. Grims weren't the king's hunting hounds like Spites were the queen's. They were worse.

With a Spite, the queen or even one of her high-ranking courtiers could call it off. That was because Spites used to be Sprites and had experience beyond the chase and the hunt.

Grims came from Umbral shadows, born of light-devouring magic, so all they ever knew was hunger. The shadow hounds ran wild and didn't answer to anyone unless a Summoner bound them, or the king blew the Hunting Horn and called them to war. Only the most strong-willed Psychics dared seek them out. Pavlo Brodsky had been near-legendary in his prime, a fact that made Richard Hopewell's subjugation of his mind one of the scariest things I knew he'd done. If he got stronger, the queen herself could be at risk from his mind magic.

We strode along for what seemed like hours until finally, a faint light appeared up ahead. I shut the quartz device off to find we'd come to the end of the thrice-accursed tunnel at last.

A rustle of leaves echoed as fresh dusk air flooded my senses. The light dimmed with Kiki's passage, and moments later, I struggled my way through some brambles and away from the entrance to the Grim Central. I followed my godmother along a deer trail, ducking in places she didn't have to in order to avoid braining myself on a branch or five. Finally, we reached a clearing. I blinked in the moonlight.

"Wait a minute." I peered at the slight incline and bare hilltop. "It's the Gnomehill again."

"Yes." Kiki literally barked. On the other side of the clearing, a bush's branches bounced. My godmother smirked, then chuckled. "I guess this Gnomehill is somehow bound to you by coincidence."

"Well, you can tell the coincidence fairy I'm getting sick of looking at it." I glared at its toadstool-ringed top.

"That's a shame." My godmother shook her head, giving me a wrung-out half-smile.

"I bet we have plenty to do, so moving along might be a good idea." I raised my eyebrows, hoping my statement was correct.

"Yes. And no." She shook her head, then hung it.

"Knowing why we have to stay this close to a whole den of Grims might be good." I put my hands on my hips.

"You'll understand in a couple of months." The Kitsune gazed up at the sky, where one star sat on the horizon.

"You have got to be kidding me, Kiki." I snorted. "Two months is a long time."

"Oh, wait." She shook her head, curls bouncing. "Not months. I've got my mortal time measurements all mixed up again. Hmm, I don't think I mean years either. Not weeks. Days might be right. Those have sixty seconds."

"Sixty seconds is a minute, Failure Godmother." I rolled my eyes.

"Oh!" She clapped her hands, seemingly immune or indifferent to my insult. "Yes! Minutes! A couple of minutes is what I mean."

"Okay, then." I nodded. "I can wait that long without curiosity killing me."

"But you shouldn't wait over here, Tony." Kiki poked my arm.

I shot her a look designed to convey the fact that I thought she might be from a planet in a whole different galaxy and blinked.

"Move about halfway up the hill, on the opposite side from where you fell through." Kiki pointed to the area she'd mentioned as if a city boy like me couldn't possibly have any sense of direction.

I headed over to the patch of earth she'd indicated, wondering about that. Because I shouldn't have been able to get my bearings in the Under. I'd never been there. So why did I know which way was North with absolute certainty? How did I understand that time moved here even though the sun never rose on the king's demesne? Did I somehow grok that time flowed the opposite way on the queen's side? Was it the whiskers, the magic, or something else?

That was one reason I was so confused. When I turned around, Kiki had vanished. I scratched my head, wondering for a moment who I'd expected to see. It was almost as though my godmother had something like the Umbral Affinity my friend Maddie did, but I'd learned to push past that since joining a pack with her in it.

"Get your brain on, Tony," I grumbled to myself. "Freaking Kitsune; shouldn't exist, and then runs off like she thinks she's Gandalf or whatev—"

I stopped complaining because there was something else that shouldn't exist—a creature that hadn't been extinct because it really was the stuff of legend. I blinked at the expanse above the Gnomehill's clearing, barely able to believe what I saw.

An angel was falling from the sky.

Olivia

Back at my room, I shooed Gee-Nome off to the lounge so I could change out of my professional outfit. I knew my royal-blue suit wasn't the usual lawyerly attire, but I'd stand out in the night court with my nearly white hair anyway. Most owl shifters had more normal-looking hair than me. Sidhe did, but they rarely tithed to the king and lived the nightlife like their Goblin counterparts. The atypically colored suit felt like armor to protect my confidence in the courtroom, the trait Mr. Ichiro said a good lawyer needed most.

As much as I loved and felt safe in my suit, I didn't want to wear it into the Under. Shifters got forced into their animal forms while visiting the Faerie realm, and our clothes didn't shift with us. I'd been surprised the night I rescued Bianca with Tony. I'd shifted, picked up her insulin in my talons, and found my clothes still on when I turned human again in the safe house, but that might have had something to do with all the crazy wards on the place. I couldn't count on that kind of thing happening again.

I had to wear something I wouldn't miss and that I could put on easily if it survived the trip once we got back. There was no way I'd do what Josh had suggested and ask Nox for help with outfitting. The Kelpie was intimidating on a good day, and tall, too. Anything she owned would drag on the floor like I was a kid playing dress-up with her mother's clothes.

Staring at the closet just wasn't the same as it had been a week before. Picking an outfit when I might run into Tony was way more exciting than dressing for utility. I settled on a long, draped midi-dress I usually wore to the beach with a big floppy sun hat. It was silvery-gray and shimmered slightly, which I always thought washed me out without the shadow of the floppy hat. I didn't care about looking monochrome on campus anymore, though.

Once I emptied my satchel of everything and slung it over my shoulder, I was ready to go. My hand on the doorknob was the only thing that kept me from jumping a mile. The whip-snap sound of a Gnome vanishing startled me at first, then the anger set in.

"You watched me, Gee. Unwise." I turned to look at the Gnome, then rushed across the room to their side and dropped to one knee. "Hoo, boy! What happened?"

"We vanish. Now." Blue blood ran from the corner of one of the poor creature's eyes. Until then, I hadn't known they bled any differently than mortal people. Gee pressed one hand over their belly, where more blood leaked. The Gnome raised their left hand and snapped their fingers.

This time, nothing happened. I gathered Gee-Nome into my arms, cradling the small faerie against my chest with no idea of what to do. Something crashed into the door. Not a knock, not a thud, a single strike. Thunder. I stood and backed toward the window. The boom came again. When the frame cracked and split, my back touched the glass.

The door fell inward, clanging against the steel headboard of my dormitory bed. The man attached to the brawny olive-toned fist snarled but stepped aside, revealing a face I wished wasn't so familiar. I could only see about two-thirds of his body since the rest was on the other side of the wall beside the broken-in door.

"Come along quietly, Miss Adler." The warm tenor and cultured accent reminded me that Gino wasn't anything like his son despite their direct relation. He flexed his hand open, and I saw something shiny up his sleeve. A projectile made of iron, perhaps?

"No." I moved one arm protectively over Gee's head. Most regular weapons bounced off Gnomes. Whatever Gino had literally up his sleeve might finish my poor friend off.

"You haven't got much choice now." He jerked his chin at the Gnome in my arms. After that, he smiled, all teeth and no warmth.

"Okay, then. Why?"

"We heard you're planning to go on the lam in the Under and

figured there must be a very good reason." Gino's grin stretched as eerily as a corpse's. "You'll tell us where you're going, of course, so we can send our own people. The king gives certain… benefits…to his champions that we don't want to miss out on."

"I'm afraid you'll miss them, then." I stared at him. "The Goblin King can tell the difference between a cat shifter and an owl shifter."

"That doesn't matter." Mr. Gitano's smile went from creepy to gleeful in under a second. Somehow, that was worse. "Unseelie rules bend. I hear he has you hunting something, and all that matters is who gets the prize first."

"Then I'll win whatever race you have planned." I felt the truth in my statement, even though I'd intended the words as a bluff. "Besides, the king clearly favors me. Rules bend in more than one way."

"But you won't even make it into the Under." The smile faded from Gino's face, displaced by stone-cold anger. "Not alive, anyway."

Gino might be right, but I wouldn't let him kill me. I opened my mouth to sass him one last time, but all that came out was a single piercing note of music. I blinked, torn between pondering what my voice box had done and getting my tailfeathers out of there. When I heard a gun cocking, I decided on the latter.

Turning my shoulder, I flung myself at the window. It cracked with only the slightest push, something entirely unexpected. Had that weird note weakened the glass like some kind of stereotypical soprano? I'd never had that happen before. Then again, I'd never willingly defenestrated myself while fleeing a man who might have been my father-in-law under different circumstances. Strange times.

There I was, plummeting five stories through the night sky without enough time to shift. I knew no glamoured trampoline was hidden below to break my fall. Tony was dead, and I'd soon join him, along with the poor Gnome who could have lived forever if the Goblin King hadn't gotten them mixed up in my business. At least we might all be together as ghosts.

"I'm sorry, Gee." I owed them an apology just in case Gnomes couldn't become ghosts after they died.

Gee groaned and stirred against my chest. I closed my eyes and waited for impact.

CHAPTER SEVEN

Olivia

I kept my mouth shut because I had no idea how high up we were after Gee vanished us from outside my dorm window. I hadn't flipped around or tumbled through the air, so the ground was at my back. The twilit sky told me it was either dawn or dusk wherever we'd gone, which was a good thing since I didn't want to be sun-blind.

The air felt strange as though I wore a backpack made of cotton candy. I couldn't figure out why my shoulders itched either. It was like I'd just finished shifting back from owl form. One look down at my arms, my Gnome friend enfolded in them, told me I was still shaped like a law student. So why did I sense the air like I was flying instead of falling?

I twisted, flipping myself over so I could try to shift in time to save Gee and me. But when I moved, the last thing I expected happened.

My wings opened, slowing our fall. I struggled to tilt them, unaccustomed to how they attached on my back with my human shoulder blades instead of without them. I screeched at the uneven drag. In girl form, my left side was stronger than my right. My owl form didn't have that problem, but these strange in-between wings sure did.

An updraft saved me. I thought for a moment I heard a song on it, but when I listened harder, the rush of air hissed and fizzled like static on an old radio. The next moment, I scanned the earth below, seeking a safe place to land. And I found a clearing with a dusty brown patch at its center and a black speck at one side. It'd do. It had to.

I wish I could say I landed on my feet on the bare earthen patch as I'd intended. I didn't. Instead, I rolled down the hill, straight for the black speck which was actually a person. Sort of. But I couldn't look closer to see whether the figure was friend or foe. Gee coughed up more of their blue blood.

"Hang in there, Gee. I'm trying to get help for you. If I only knew what you needed."

"Home." The Gnome managed that one word, but I had a problem. "Get me there."

"I wish I knew where you lived, Gee." My throat felt full of cotton and my eyes like the lake side of a dam.

"Um, not that I know anything, but maybe they live in the Gnomehill."

"What?" I didn't dare look up. The voice sounded exactly like Tony's. Could it be him, alive? Or was he a ghost? I stared at my hands then at Gee. Would my hopes be dashed to bits like Icarus on the rocks?

My knees rested on the ground, the dry autumn grass itching through the thin fabric of my dress. I didn't want to look, wasn't sure I could bear seeing Tony's ghost right now. If I didn't look, maybe I could pretend it wasn't him.

"I said, maybe the Gnomehill you're sitting on is Gee-Nome's actual house. In which case, we want to get them in there so their clan can help them heal from whatever's killing them right now."

"Right." I stood and walked toward the hole in the bare earth on the other side of the toadstools. I stepped right in, trusting my wings to slow my fall, and landed with barely a jostle.

My eyes adjusted to the darkness quickly. I was in a round chamber and could see two sets of footprints in a coating of thick dust, meaning that some other people had been in here recently. Passageways led off in two directions. Both had those footprints, but one of them gave me the creeps. I was about to head down the less shadowy hallway when Gee groaned.

"Ahead." The Gnome gasped, shuddering against my arm. "The wall."

I nodded, then walked forward until I got to the far side of the chamber. With my owl vision, I saw a small doorway in the stonework at the height of my head. I reached up and knocked because I couldn't think of anything else a sane person would do in a situation like this.

The little door opened, swinging silently outward on nothing I could see. No voice greeted Gee or challenged me. A sullen glow came from the other side of the tiny threshold.

"In." Gee's voice sounded faint and strained. I set them just inside the door, and it swung shut just as quietly as it had opened. After that, I heard the stamp of diminutive feet from where they were.

"It won't kill you to look at me, Olivia." I couldn't pretend any longer. That was definitely Tony talking.

"Maybe, but I don't want to see you dead and trapped in the Under." I shuddered. "That's got to be where we are since Gnomehills don't exist in the mortal world."

"I'm not dead." Tony's gruff chuckle made my breath catch in my chest. It came from above me. "I'm getting better."

"No, you're not." The lines from the old British movie poured from my mouth as inevitably as rain. "You've been stone-dead all week." I froze as I heard the patter of falling earth, canvas rustle, and a scraping thud behind me. Ghosts didn't make noises like that.

"I feel fine." Tony's voice echoed in the chamber. Did ghostly voices make echoes? Three steps sounded behind me. "I think I'll go for a walk. Come on, Olivia, turn around already. You can't avoid looking at me forever."

I couldn't answer. The only way I could be sure of anything was to turn around and face him as he asked. But now, I didn't want to for a completely different reason. My face was dirt-smudged and tear-stained, and I knew from long experience that I was an ugly crier.

"I don't want you to see me like this."

"Like what?"

"I'm a mess."

"Like hell. I thought you looked like something while you fell out of the sky, and a mess wasn't it. Anyway, you can't be more of a wreck than the time you smacked into the side of a building on Camp Street, and I had to carry you home. And there's no way you're ickier than when Hopewell's construct slimed you in Water Place Park. I outgrew the idea that girls have cooties a long time ago, too."

"Um, well. It's just—"

"Okay. So, maybe you don't want to look at me. I don't blame you. After all the run around I've given you, I wouldn't want to look at me—"

"Hoo, boy." I turned on my heel and flung myself at him.

Most people would expect physical grace from two people who shifted into stealthy predators. They might think meeting the man you secretly love after thinking he was dead automatically blossoms into some sort of grand romantic scene. Most people would be wrong on both counts.

He swept me off my feet, but only because I tripped over his. We tumbled together, but not in a swooning, sexy, or even roughhousing fun way. Tony ended up on his back with the wind knocked out of him, and one arm twisted behind him. I sprawled across his chest, my lower lip somehow busted from smacking his chin. *The Notebook*, it was not.

"You're alive, Tony Gitano." I turned my head and set my ear against his chest just to be sure. "Yup. Heartbeat and everything. I bet you were only mostly dead."

"Heh. Because mostly dead is slightly alive." Tony hacked out a cough. "Don't go through my clothes looking for loose change, now."

I lifted my head so I could see his face. He smirked with the left side of his mouth and his right eyebrow lifted. I had to put my hands over my own mouth to muffle my impending laughter. That expression, combined with the ears sticking up on top of his head, would have looked at home in an anime. He tilted his head, reminding me that he'd ultimately turned down my most direct advances.

"Never mind." I rolled off of him, then shook my head. "You sound way too lively for me to make that kind of mistake." I stood and dusted myself off, then leaned down to give him a hand up.

"Good call." Tony pushed himself up on his elbows. He didn't try to get up or reach for my hand. Instead, he just sort of half sat there, looking up at me. "Olivia Adler, you're the last person I expected to see in a place like this. I'm not complaining because you're a sight for sore eyes. But what's a nice owl like you doing in a place like the king's side of the Under?"

"I'm supposed to be at the heart of it, actually." I peered down the less creepy of the two passageways. "His hunting lodge, to be more specific."

"You can't get into that club without an invitation."

"Oh, I had one."

"Wow." Tony blinked. "I mean, even Duke Ismail can't get his mitts on one of those unless it's a full-court occasion."

"He said he had a Quest for me." I shrugged, looking at the floor. I made my way down the less creepy hallway.

"A Quest." Tony padded along behind me. "Faeries don't usually give Quests to shifters."

"Well, the king gave one to me."

"How in the name of all things holy did you get to meet the Goblin King?"

"At your memorial service."

"Huh." Tony didn't bump into me when I stopped at the end of the hall, so that must have meant he'd stopped, too. "You're supposed to be at the hunting lodge, but you ended up on a Gnomehill. Weird."

"Well, that's what happens when a mortally injured Gnome has to vanish someone at gunpoint."

"Whoever threatened you is getting a faceful of claws from yours truly." I heard his knuckles crack behind me. Who was it?"

"Your dad."

I didn't want to have a conversation as serious as this one was shaping up to be in the dark, even if we could both sort of see in it. I stepped ahead into what I hoped was a chamber with some torches I could light. The room did me one better. Magical braziers flickered on, apparently sensing my presence. I stopped and stared.

The first thing I felt was nostalgia like I'd been in this room before. Déjà vu was too weak a term for the way this place moved me. Something in the air ruffled my feathers, familiarity in a foreign place. I paced across to one of the dusty tapestries, noting that the floor's own dust had a single set of footprints in it, unmistakably the imprint of Converse All-Stars in Tony's size.

I would have asked Tony what he'd been doing in here before, or what he might know about the place. But though my mind teemed with questions, I couldn't give them a voice until I'd checked this one panel of fabric draped over the wall. That's how much the muted images and ambiance of that room had gotten its hooks into me.

With one hand, I brushed the surface in slow-motion, clearing part of the image woven into the fabric. After that, I worked faster, uncovering the whole thing.

A woman with prismatic wings faced east as she soared over a nest strewn with shards of eggs. Another ran into the west on the ground below, a bundle under her arms. The running woman was all dressed in red with a scarf tied around the top of her head. Long red hair and waves that might have been scarves or tails streamed out behind her like comets. The flying woman held a green bow, strung and nocked with arrows. She pointed them at a line of figures on the horizon, possibly an advancing army.

"This tapestry shows a story I've heard before." I scratched my head. "But I don't know which one."

"I didn't even know there were pictures on these things." Tony gazed at the image along with me, his eyes lingering on the lady in red. They widened as he looked more closely at the flying woman's weapon. "That lady with the wings is one of the legendary birds of the Under. And I can tell by the rainbow wings that she's the Alkonost."

"I've never heard of them." I studied the woman's face, wishing the image had been done in a clearer medium than needlepoint on fabric.

"There are three. The Alkonost is Seelie, the Sirin is Unseelie, and the Gamayun is Switzerland."

I chuckled, but the mirth his quip inspired faded quickly. Standing on my toes, I stretched up to reach the embroidered wings. I had to know more but didn't know where to start asking.

"They're even more extinct than Kitsune." Tony stepped beside me, peering up at the fabric under my hand. "In order to have a shot at becoming one of the birds, you have to be born in the Under. None of the PPC professors has even seen one, and some of them are faeries with long lives."

"But this only looks like a couple of decades of dust." I glanced sideways at him, a shiver of certainty starting in my gut and working its way out through the rest of my body. "Who'd have stitched something like this twenty some odd years ago?"

"Whoever hid this, I guess." He held out a burlap-wrapped parcel. "I didn't understand when I came in here before. This place gave me the heebie-jeebies, like a goose walking over my grave. But I think I get it now." He glanced at my wings, their monochrome tones nothing like the embroidered Alkonost's rainbow-hued ones. His smile startled me with the implication that he might like mine better. "I think this crazy artifact is meant for you, not me."

"Um, thanks, I guess."

"Aren't you going to open it?"

"I already know it's a bow, arrows too."

"Gotta love the smart chicks."

I turned to look at him, smiling, and our eyes met. Something about being in this room with Tony felt familiar, too. Right, somehow. Like we were home, in a sense, even though I thought we'd never been alone in a Gnomehill before. I wasn't sure what to say or do or whether I needed to do or say anything. The moment hung like a Rembrandt, and then, Tony decided the art show was over. He closed one of his hands around my upper arm and headed for the exit.

"We should get out of here." Tony faced the door, his whiskers twitching.

"Why?"

"The non-Gnomish residents of this place are due to wake up soon." He wrinkled his nose. "They're Grims."

"Plural?" I blinked at his nod. "That sucks."

"We'll have to sneak past them, too. They've infested the other tunnel, and the only exit's at the end of it." He stopped, pulling on my arm to hold me back. "Crap on a crap cracker. It's too late for that."

There, right in the middle of the Gnomehill's main chamber, stood a pack of Grims.

"Don't worry." I turned, pressing the wrapped bow between us so I could hold Tony in a secure grip. "I've got this."

There weren't any drafts at all, but that didn't matter. The main chamber was big enough for me to open my wings, so I beat my wings, building my own wind beneath them. I hadn't accounted for the extra weight. Moving us out of there turned out to be a bigger feat of physical strength than I'd expected. It took longer than I would have liked, but our feet lifted off the floor.

The Grims started toward us, but one advantage to lifting both of us was the amount of downdraft I'd kicked up. The gale buffeted the Grims, making them misjudge their leaps and pounces.

One of them snagged the hem of Tony's coat in its teeth. Tony kicked it in the nose, sending the Grim falling back down to the stone floor. It made no sound as it landed, no smack of flesh on the rock, not even a whimper or whine. That was the creepy thing about the Umbral hounds. They were sentient but not exactly a living force. Shadows never were.

Once I'd flown us out of the hole, things got easier. The king's side of the Under had plenty of currents in its skies for me to work with. Soon, we soared over trees and even a few other clearings. My wings and back burned with the strain, so I landed us on the shore of what looked like an ocean.

"Well, that's the weirdest water I've ever seen." Tony stepped back before the next wave broke against the drab sand. "Whoever heard of a beach like this?"

"Goblins, apparently." I dipped one toe in the water, then pulled it back. The purple water was freezing cold. It stained the sand it had touched black, although farther up, it was slate gray. "At least it's not blue and pink like cotton candy."

"It is out that way." Tony jerked his chin toward the east. "Queen's demesne is a different scene."

"No more rhymes now. I mean it."

"Sorry, I'm all out of peanuts."

I couldn't take any more. At that point, I couldn't bring myself to care about my botched arrival in the Under or pissing off a Faerie monarch or even that somewhere in the mortal realm, Gino Gitano was trying to get here and wanted me dead. Tony was alive, and I was with him. I did the only thing I could.

I laughed.

CHAPTER EIGHT

Tony

Olivia's laugh sounded like the bells at the little chapel I used to go to with Dad before he got tired of pretending at his religion. I'd hidden there many times, once I learned to shift, pretending to be some kind of church cat. Whenever I needed to get out of the path of one of Dad's rages, it'd been my haven, the only place I felt safe. But there was something else in Olivia's laugh besides comfort and a sense of safety.

She bent my heart like a prism bends light, transforming it in ways even a shifter like me wasn't accustomed to. I couldn't handle something that intense, so I stood and turned, facing away from her to gaze out at the dark western horizon. I realized I'd avoided asking her direct questions ever since she'd gotten there. After Olivia had laughed, that didn't feel right anymore.

I'd spent most of my life either looking over my shoulder or wondering when the other shoe would drop. I barely ever looked ahead. For me, nothing was a "glass half-full or half-empty" proposition. I'm the kind of guy who wonders whether the liquid is water or sulfuric acid. It sounds Emo, but Olivia Adler's laughter broke my feelings into pieces and refracted from them until I feared what they might become. I did the only thing I could in that situation.

I turned around and cleared my throat.

"Hmm?" Olivia tilted her head, peering up at me. Her silvery-white hair tumbled around her bare shoulders. Maybe it was just my weird opinion, but no other woman I knew could look like she'd been in a salon instead of dragging my mangy carcass out of a Grim's den.

"So, we've got to get to the king's hunting lodge?" Being able to just flat-out ask a simple question felt like drinking ice water on a midsummer day.

"Yeah." Olivia nodded. "At least, I have to. You don't."

"But I will." I crossed my arms over my chest. "You've got an honest-to-goodness Quest, like one of the king's knights. So, you should also have someone helping you."

"The king sent Gee to help me." Olivia fixed me with a defiant stare.

"Well, he's sidelined." I stared right back. "You're stuck with the not-really-dead guy."

"I can live with that." Olivia blinked, breaking the stare and my challenge of her reluctance to accept my help. She stood up and brushed black sand off her dress. "We have no idea where the hunting lodge is, so I'll shift to owl form and scout it out. After that, I'll get back in this form, and you can turn into a cat. It's easier to carry you that way."

"Okay. Sounds like a solid plan." I nodded. Olivia wouldn't be able to fly any distance dragging me along while I was this size.

"Um, would you mind turning around?" A delicate shade of pink touched her cheekbones as she lifted an empty satchel off her shoulder.

"Oh!" My face heated despite the cool breeze. She'd have to take her clothes off to shift. "Um, right." I turned around, treating my eyes to the dark western horizon again. I tried meditation to empty my mind of the images it conjured. My imagination didn't want to cooperate. I decided to let my mind wander where it wanted to go. And that's why I didn't react the first time I heard it.

"Tony!" Olivia's voice sounded strained and desperate, something that went along with the pictures in my head. "Tony." The second time, she said my name with a hint of despair. That got my real-time attention. I turned around to see what was wrong.

"Holy mother of cats—"

Olivia Adler, the woman of my dreams, stood on the beach in the altogether, and I was utterly undone. Had I thought she'd looked angelic falling from the sky with a wounded Gnome in her arms? I'd been wrong. Here was the real angel. She moved her hands to cover herself, and my perception shifted to imagine her as Botticelli's Venus rising from the sea.

If I'd been honorable like Boy Scout Bobby the bear shifter, I'd have looked away. If I'd been chivalrous like my bestie, Sir Fred Redford of the queen's court, I'd have handed over my trench coat without staring. And if I'd been a rogue like Blaine Harcourt, I might have taken her right there on the beach. But I was and always will be Tony Gitano, paranoid neighborhood cat-man. My reactions consisted of flight and fright. Fright won. I froze.

I couldn't move, couldn't even blink. It was as if the sight of her had turned me into a pillar of salt. I sure felt sinful enough to be one at that moment. And then, Olivia moved her hands, putting them on her hips. My heart made a mad dash like a last-ditch sprinter. I expected a slap in the face at best and a nasty left hook at worst. I got neither.

"We've got a problem, Tony." Olivia rolled her shoulders. Her wings flapped, kicking up sand from the dry dunes behind me. After that, they folded over her, hiding the view. "I can't shift. And I don't know if it's this place or just me."

I tried to say something. Anything. I knew the problem, of course. Olivia was a magical shifter of some unknown variety, just like me. But all I could do was open and close my mouth. I wondered if this was how fish shifters would act if they existed.

"Have you tried shifting since you got here?" A tiny crease formed between Olivia's eyebrows.

"No." I sighed. "Actually, I don't know, but probably not. Supposedly, I've been here a whole week, and I only remember less than half of this day."

"Hoo, boy." Usually, she'd make me laugh or at least smirk with that utterance, but her tone tumbled like a waterfall. Tears did the same, from those wide amber eyes of hers. It was just too much.

"Forget about it." I took a step forward, patting one side of her wing. I blinked at how insubstantial that limb of bone and feathers felt under my hand. Fragile. Had they really carried the both of us through the air? I owed her, even if it wasn't in the faerie "three questions" sense. "Look, I'll try now, though. For you."

She blinked then swallowed. Olivia's tears hadn't dried up. Humidity levels on a beach went against the chances of that, even in the Under. But she'd stopped adding to them, at least.

I took a deep breath and concentrated on calling my cat form. Other shifters, guys like Bobby and Josh, or even gals like Jeannie and Beth, treated their animal forms almost like another person or maybe a character they'd have played on TV. I didn't. Those others loved being magical, having another body to inhabit once in a while. Maybe they found it empowering. My cat form felt good-for-nothing, embarrassing, and puny, just like Dad always told me. I used it primarily to hide.

Turning into a relatively little kitty cat shortly after my voice cracked had been a major disappointment for my parental unit. I'd always thought I was the reason Dad had bumped Mom off. Never mind that she'd died before I could remember her. All the same, my fluffy Maine Coon form had caused me no end of pain and trouble. Magic was fascinating, Faerie intriguing, and

Psychic powers a nifty curiosity. Being a regular shifter had always felt like a bum deal.

Anyway, I didn't bother disrobing. My literally little friend wouldn't do anything to my clothes besides leave behind tufts of shed fur, not even enough for a hairball. I called on that puny cat form, cursing it inside my head the entire time as usual. But this time, it didn't come. I twitched my tail and flicked my ears.

"You too, huh?" Olivia shook her head. "And that whole shifting and flying thing was my plan B, too. I'm all out of options."

"Well, what about just walking up the beach instead?" I shrugged. "You never know, maybe the king likes oceanfront property."

"The trouble with that is, we're out in the open." Olivia looked over my shoulder, her eyes moving left, then right. She lowered her voice. "I'm not sure if you noticed, but we're being watched. What if they follow us?"

"Maybe they're watching because two half-shifted people are on a beach, and one of them is, um, well..." I waved a hand at her and looked down at my shoes.

"Oh." She kept looking at the tree line. I wasn't sure whether she was that afraid or meant to avoid looking me in the eye. "Well, I'm not sure about that. Your father kind of said he'd try to get my Quest done before I could. What if it's him?"

"Oh, really?" I smacked my fist against my other hand. Then, I reached down and grabbed the burlap bundle. "Well, I've got just the thing for that. A long-range weapon."

"You did not bring a gun into the Under." She shook her head, eyes wide.

"No way I'd go and do something like that." I unwrapped the fabric, revealing the weapon. "It's magical, and I found it here. Problem is, I have no idea how to use this thing."

"Ooh!" Olivia's mouth went as round as her eyes. "Archery

was my extracurricular all through middle and high school. Give it here."

I handed the bow over. Olivia bounced up and down a little, flapping her wings as she examined the length of greenish wood and its accessories. She bent and strung it in seconds. I blinked, even more impressed with watching her handle a lethal weapon in the nude than when she'd just been standing there. I still couldn't look away.

"Um, you might want to get dressed at some point." I tried to keep my eyes on the bow, but that cause was lost before it even started. I covered my eyes instead.

"Hoo, boy!"

I heard a rustle of fabric, waited for the sound to stop before taking my hands away.

"Thanks, Tony." Olivia ran her hands over the carved wood of the now bent short bow. "This is the nicest bow I've ever seen. Feels like it was made just for me. Where did it come from?"

I'd have snarked back at almost anyone else asking a question like that. But Olivia didn't make the words sound doubtful or accusatory like I'd somehow lied to her or stolen the thing. Even though technically speaking, I had sort of borrowed it.

"The Gnomehill. The whole reason I was even there in the first place was to fetch the thing."

"Oh! Are you on a Quest, too?"

"I'm not really sure?" I shrugged. "It's just that this...um, well, it turns out that someone was with me when I woke up."

"Really?" She raised an eyebrow. "Who?"

"I guess I have a godmother I never knew about. She said the bow was the only way forward for me." I shrugged. "Apparently, it's my bane, so I shouldn't be using it myself, anyway."

"So, your faerie godmother said you needed to get this." Olivia nocked an arrow to the bow and sighted along it. "But why?"

"Well, I guess it's going to be useful in, um, eliminating

someone from Richard Hopewell's camp." Somehow, admitting that was almost harder than watching her stand there naked.

She kept the bow ready, then headed up the beach like I'd suggested. "Your dad."

I blinked, expecting a question instead of a statement. "Well, yeah."

"Good." Her smile reminded me of ice. She eased the string back, removing the arrow from it.

"He must have done more than threaten you, then."

"Unfortunately for him, yes." Olivia examined the arrow. Its tip was wood, carved to a point, and etched with vaguely Cyrillic symbols.

"So he's the one who put a hole in Gee-Nome?" I glanced down at her dress, the dark blue stains there reminding me of the Gnome's injuries.

"I think so. If he didn't, it was one of his people." Olivia put the arrow away, then slung the quiver over her shoulder. Somehow, the strap adjusted to her wings. I thought about how the winged woman on the tapestry had worn it. This looked almost the same.

"You know I'm one of his people, too."

"No." She shook her head and looked me right in the eyes. "You might be his son, but you're not one of his people."

But Olivia was wrong about that. I'd done things, stained my hands with my father's dirty deeds. It'd been under what a lawyer might call extreme duress. All the same, I wasn't sure Olivia's faith in me could wash any of that clean. Before I could challenge her assumption, something caught my eye at the tree-line. I turned my head and stopped in my tracks.

The sky above had purpled like a bruise the entire time I'd been in the Under. With the shadow of the trees, it turned into that sick yellow-green that comes a week later. Maybe that was why the light off in the distance looked so intriguing. Or maybe it just reminded me of a laser pointer. I'm a cat shifter, so I can't help myself sometimes. Maybe the partial shift and the Faerie realm's magic brought more of my feline instincts to the surface.

Anyway, I headed in that direction. That's a lie. I leaped and bounded in a straight line. The only thing that slowed me down was the dried-out dunes at the head of the beach. The sand dragged at my shoes, but my feet didn't care. They kept on going.

"Tony, come back!"

I tried to stop, but my legs moved anyway. My mind and heart wanted me to stop, but my body just wouldn't.

I did the only thing I could do in that situation.

I quoted another movie.

CHAPTER NINE

Olivia

"Somebody stop me!" Tony's voice tightened to near-breaking. I'd packed up my pride when it came to Tony Gitano and his zany reactions, but I would not abide him running away from me in abject terror. Not after he'd seen me naked.

I leaped into the air, flapping my wings. I wanted speed, not altitude. Luckily for me, the beach was windy in my favor, so it wasn't too difficult. On the way, I glimpsed what had caught Tony's attention. A will-o'-the-wisp.

I landed scant feet short of the tree line and spun on my heel, pointing the bow upward. It tingled with magic energy as I stood in Tony's way. We collided and tumbled to the sandy hardpan that marks the landward edge of any shoreline.

As I fell, I loosed my arrow. I heard it hiss through the underbrush.

"Oh, nooooooooooooooo!" After that came a strung-out squeak like air slowly releasing from a balloon's neck.

I turned my head, peering through bushes with freshly tattered leaves. With a will-o'-the-wisp around, that was hardly a good idea. I breathed a sigh overdue enough to inspire a library hold. My arrow had pinned the wisp to a tree. It looked as deflated as a wet poodle and more dismayed than a dairy-allergic kid at an ice cream social.

"Thanks." Tony stood over me, one flat palm stretched toward my free arm.

"No, thanks to you." I let him help me up, so I didn't have to drop my mysterious new weapon.

"You're a hoot, you know that?" He smirked.

"Hoo, boy. You know, I've never ever heard a joke like that before in my entire life, Tony." I rolled my eyes. Just to make things fair, I dropped him a wink. "Be right back, have to get that arrow." I started off toward the tree where something that looked like a deflated and glittery blueberry hung against pale birch bark.

"It's dangerous, getting that close to a Will-o'-the-wisp, Olivia."

"I know." I shrugged, looking down as I tried to navigate crackly underbrush in flip-flops and a progressively snagged maxi-dress. "But there's something about this weapon's magic. It feels different from other magipsychic devices. And I'm not going to risk leaving an arrow behind where anyone can find it. I don't want to give whoever's watching us any literal ammunition."

I turned my head halfway over my shoulder, glaring off into the trees toward the south, where I sensed the presence of something breathing. Tony flicked an ear in that direction, his tail twitching. His nostrils flared, and his whiskers shook. He mouthed a word, something with an "o" between two consonants. I wasn't sure what he'd meant, but as long as he hadn't scented his father, I didn't much care.

I jerked my chin at the item I'd pinned to the tree, which was definitely not a Will-o'-the-wisp. That Unseelie creature had already made their escape. Somebody had tied a shiny blue ribbon on it, and that's what my shot had snagged. That was all right by me. I had no idea what to do with a captive Wisp, anyway.

"Yeah, you should get the arrow. But Olivia," Tony kicked at a clump of fallen leaves. He stayed back, not looking at the tree. "There's something else about that bow you don't—"

"Ye knaves!" The thing pinned to the tree spoke. Its voice sounded tinny and far-off, child-like, too. "Scurvy rapscallions! I'll have you walk the plank!"

"Um, excuse me, but manners are a thing." I grabbed the arrow. "Use them."

"But, but I'm a pirate!" I could practically hear the pout. "We're supposed to talk like this."

"Yeah, right." Tony snorted. "A will-o'-the-wisp pirate. Now I've heard everything."

"But I am one! I'm the first mate, my mama says so!"

"Um, you've taken this pretend-y pirate adventure game too far now." Tony leaned on one hand against the tree. "Everyone knows wisps don't have parents."

"Tony, this isn't a will-o'-the-wisp." I yanked the arrow free. The blue thing fell to the ground, and I pointed at it. "Have a closer look."

"Huh." Tony bent over and peered down. "Magipsychic device. Some kind of spyware, I think. But who'd cover a magical bugging device in blue glitter and tie it to one of the most obnoxious pure faeries in the known universe?"

"Hello, sir at the other end of this magipsychic device." I knew the reason this new voice had better manners. I recognized who it belonged to. Tony didn't, or acted like he didn't, at least.

"Hello," he said. "You must be Captain Mom."

"And you sound like Tony Gitano, but you can't be. He passed away last week."

"Yeah, he did. Hold on." Tony pulled a scrap of black fabric from a pocket, picked the device up with it, and held it out to me.

"Hi, Gemma." I couldn't help but smile. Gemma Tolland was a troll from one of the oldest and highest-ranking families in the king's court. Back in the mundane world, she ran a salvage boat with her grandfather. "Wow, you told me before you had more rank and responsibilities in the Under than the knights, but I'd never have guessed that meant commanding your own ship."

"Olivia Adler?" Gemma's chuckle sounded like a babbling brook. "How did you get tangled up in the other end of my kid's mischief?"

"It's a long story." I stowed the arrow in its quiver and slung the bow across my back.

"It's not mischief, Mom!" A swooshing sound garbled the child's voice, but I managed to make out the rest. "Was trying to scout the beach for enemies, is all."

"Wait a minute." Gemma took a deep breath, then sighed it out. "Are you on the beach? In the Under? How did you get here?"

That was when one of the most curious things happened. I felt something wash over my body, a ripple of energy. Silence on the other end of the line told me Gemma had felt it, too.

"No way." Tony blinked at the glitter-encrusted surveillance device. "There is no way that just happened."

"Tell me where you are, and I will pick you up." Gemma lowered her voice. "Don't talk to anyone before I get there, no matter what."

I told her, keeping my voice to a near whisper. The last thing I wanted to do was piss off my literal mom-friend.

I turned, looked back the way we'd come. The sun touched the sea at the horizon, mixing hues across the water's surface like an oil slick. But there wasn't any oil in the Under. That's just how light and darkness behaved there. Tony gazed out, too. His black-furred tail flicked, and his matching ears flattened nearly against his skull.

"Are you pondering what I'm pondering?"

"There's no time for *Animaniacs* quotes." Tony tilted his head, somehow managing to look at me sideways and down his nose all at the same time. "You need to tell me why you got a faerie magic surge when Gemma asked you three questions and didn't when I made the same mistake."

"Mistake?" I blinked. "I wouldn't ever hold you to faerie rules, Tony. You know me better than that."

"You might not want to, but we're in the Under." Tony shook his head, then turned to face me with his hands on his hips. "It's faerie law and nothing else in this neck of the woods, so tell me, already."

"But I don't know." I sighed. "I felt it, Gemma felt it. But I have no idea what it even means. You have to remember, all I know about magic is what's legal in the mundane world with and without a permit and what kind of punishment extrahumans get for breaking the laws there. I've never even felt magic that didn't come from a gadget before."

"But you've been seeing ghosts ever since you went nocturnal." Tony put one hand in his pocket. I tilted my head, peering. It was the front pocket in his jeans, not one of the many in his trench coat.

"Yeah, mediumship's a Psychic ability, not magic. And anyway, we already talked about that." I glanced at his face, and my cheeks heated. Not in the fun I-have-a-crush-on-you way I usually got around Tony Gitano, either. I couldn't help it, I was about to have an angry cry right there in the king's demesne. "Told you we should have let the rest of the pack in on that, but did you listen?"

"No. And I should have." Tony's tail drooped. "I've been lying to them for way too long, and maybe for the wrong reasons. And I'm sorry. Especially for the way it's affected you, Olivia."

We stood like that for a moment, then I took a step toward him. He froze, so I didn't take another. I don't know why I'd risk embarrassing myself by throwing myself at him again like I had at the spring party. He'd already made it clear that he wasn't interested enough.

"Anyway, Tony, I wish I knew more about magic than the legalese." I felt the first tear escape the corner of my eye and make its way down the side of my nose. The fact that I couldn't control my tears when I got angry only magnified the feeling. "I'm worse than useless down here, and you deserve better help."

"Wait, what? I deserve—" Tony coughed. Then he smacked the side of his face with one hand. "You're worried about helping me, and you're the one on the Quest. Look, all I really want right now is just some honest truth from anyone willing to give it. You're already helping, in case you forgot about the legendary bow you're carrying, which I am unable to use without shooting my eye out."

"Legendary bow?"

"Yeah." Tony rolled his eyes. "Dammit. You're packing crazy powerful faerie bow heat. Of course, you're getting whacked-out faerie magic effects. And there's the answer to my freaking question. Right under my nose."

"I don't know, Tony." I pressed my lips together, thinking back to the moment right before Gee had vanished us into the Under. The way my voice had weakened the glass felt magical too, and that didn't come from the bow or the Under.

"Of course, you don't. Because there's more about that bow that I haven't told you."

"And there's more about how I got to the Under that I didn't tell you, either."

"Guess we're both guilty—"

"As charged."

"Hey, stop finishing my sentences!"

"At least I'm not finishing your sandwiches."

"I wouldn't care if you did. Do I look like a Redcap to you?" Tony rolled his eyes. I glanced at his tail. It stood up again, its end curved gently into a shape resembling a question mark. His ears stood up, too, turned toward me.

"Look, Tony. I think I broke my dorm window while jumping out of it."

"Not unusual."

"And I don't even like Tom Jones. That's Mom's music." I had to seriously restrain myself from bursting into song, though. The tunes you grow up hearing in the background tend to stick, even when you don't want them to. "Seriously. I didn't touch the glass. It shattered when I opened my mouth, and some weird music came out when I tried to scream at your father."

"Well, then." Tony's left eyebrow arched. "My theory's probably impossible, but it might explain how you managed to hit the magipsychic bug and scare off the will-o'-the-wisp even though I'd knocked you flat on your back."

"What do you mean?"

"Magic owl girl." He jerked his chin at me. "Legendary Faerie bow." He pointed at the weapon slung across my shoulder. "That bow, string, and quiver are the Goblin King's Garters."

I opened my mouth to say something, I forget what. A crackle of twigs and leaves underfoot sounded instead of my voice. We turned in tandem to see Gemma Tolland standing just past the tree line.

"Thought I sensed a major magical force here." Gemma's arms crossed over her chest, hands hovering over her pistol on the left and rapier on the right. She drew the flintlock weapon and pointed it at Tony. "I'll help you kill the doppelgänger if you clear my debt, Olivia."

"Um, no." I shook my head and stepped in front of Tony. "He's no such thing."

"Yeah, Gemma. I'm the real deal."

"Prove it." Gemma lifted the pistol, aiming over my head. "Tell me something only Tony knows."

"I know your kid's dad. He's on the wrong side as far as you're concerned."

Gemma Tolland didn't drop her weapon, but I thought it was

a near thing. She managed to holster the pistol after one failed attempt. The captain beckoned with one hand, reminding me of someone telling us to "bring it." After that, she spun on the heel of one knee-high boot and strode back through the trees and onto the beach.

We followed, spying a tall ship flying an antlered Jolly Roger in the distance. A dinghy waited for us, aground at the shoreline.

CHAPTER TEN

Tony

I got into the dinghy. I hated large bodies of water with the fire of a thousand suns. But if the troll thought there was something as strong as a Doppelgänger around, I believed her. So did Olivia, apparently. She climbed aboard, too. It didn't occur to me at the time that all that magic might have come from us.

Gemma rowed on her own, barking commands to what looked like a rudder that moved all by itself. But I wasn't fooled. I knew a sea nymph when I saw one, which only ever happened in peripheral vision for most people, myself included. So I almost waved at the purple-haired faerie, so that Gemma understood I knew she wasn't alone on the boat with us.

I stopped myself and stuck my hands in my pockets. Why should I threaten one of the king's captains, anyway? She owed Olivia a favor, and neither had agreed that a ride in an Unseelie Pirate ship would repay it. Any bravado I whipped out would just look like a dick move.

I sat in the swaying dinghy with my eyes half-closed, trying not to think about all the surrounding water. That let in the idea that my first impulse had been to act like a thug. I pictured a big, heavy boot kicking the self-hatred overboard with cement over-shoes. It wore Armani, like Dad. The corners of my mouth refused to tilt up, but at least I'd cleared a little patch for myself in the old psyche.

Avoiding my issues worked just fine all the way to the ship. It kept right on working as we stepped on board, and all the way down into what I assumed were the captain's quarters. The door was red and ornately carved. That Unseelie Jolly Roger grinned down at us, the horns more like a stag's antlers close up and without wind distorting the picture. Gemma's hand grasped the brass doorknob, twisted until it clicked, and pulled the door open.

We stepped inside to see a grizzled old man, a troll by his tusks and braided fauxhawk, engaged in a play-duel with a small child wearing an oversized bicorn hat. She giggled as she stepped under his thrust and tagged him on the belly with a curved wooden sword.

"Ack! Ya got me!" The older gent made a totally fake hacking sound as he collapsed to his knees. "Bested by a wee scalawag!"

"Haha, Grampa!" The kid danced from one foot to the other, waving her hands. The hat tilted, revealing a shock of tangerine hair. I saw her mistake. She'd left her entire torso exposed. "Oh, noooooo!"

The old troll grabbed her and pulled her close. He stood, sweeping her up in the air as he rose. Then he drew her soft, exposed belly toward his tusked mouth. My stomach dropped like an elevator with the cord cut.

"Kid—" I reached out, about to stop what my imagination whispered would happen next.

But it didn't.

A fit of giggles floated over the sound of one enormous and wet raspberry.

I stood there with my hand out like the biggest idiot in the Under. I knew well what my damage was. The Tolland family had nothing like it. My knee-jerk reaction assumed Gramps would do something vindictive, show her up, take her down a notch. Maybe even hurt her. I'd seen Magi, vampires, faeries, and a zoo's worth of shifter types all my life. I'd even started seeing ghosts recently. But my eyes had gone almost twenty-four years without taking in anything like the kind of love between that little girl and her Grandpa.

I stared, not sure I could believe in any of it. A cold knowledge touched my heart like a pebble on a headstone. All this time, I thought love like that just didn't exist. It was fake, maybe, like Bigfoot or the Loch Ness Monster. And really, I'd been wrong. I just wasn't destined to experience love like that myself.

I understood how humans managed, denying the existence of all things magical for ages. When you're not part of something special, it breaks your heart hard enough to slam the door on reality. That's why people fail to believe the truth, even when it's right in front of them. Denying it hurts less.

Something warm and soft closed over my fist with the pointing finger. I couldn't hold my arm up anymore, but the gentle weight helped me ease it down instead of dropping it. I looked down and to the right.

"It's okay, Tony." Olivia's voice didn't just speak the words. Something in that utterance sounded like a song, one that held the door open for me.

Denial might hurt less, but in the long run, it costs way too much. I looked back at the loving family, fixed my eyes on them as they laughed together like a starving stray might on a square meal. Love existed. Somebody had it. Maybe love was an element, like the water the Galleon sailed on. Water didn't make excuses for its presence or absence. Why should love? And who was I to judge something like the ocean, anyway?

"I'd better introduce you all." Gemma reached for the child

and settled her on one hip before planting a kiss on her forehead, right above the kid's left eyebrow. "This is my daughter, Hope. And that's my Grandfather, Admiral John Tolland." She extended a hand at Olivia and introduced her formally, first and last name and all.

"Um, what about Tony?" Olivia fixed her gaze on Gemma, a look that was a hair shy of being a glare.

"Like I said, I'm not a hundred percent sure that's Tony."

"Oh, come on, Gemma." I rolled my eyes. "I gave you some private intel."

"It wasn't enough to be sure." The captain of the paranoia ship shook her head. "Dad, give him the doppelgänger test."

"Right." The admiral reached in his pocket, then turned to look down at me. He couldn't help it. That's just what happens when a guy who's six-three and at least two eighty faces a dude under five-eight and one seventy-five.

John Tolland pulled his hand from his pocket and raised it closed around something. He pointed it at me the same way a dude-bro might when expecting a fist bump. I just stood there, not sure what was happening or what I could do about it if he decided to haul off and break my nose for the seventeenth time. But he did no such thing. That doesn't mean it didn't hurt.

"Ow!" A blinding flare of light sort of like those old-fashioned photo flashbulbs knocked my eyesight right out. Waves of red and brown streaked across blobs of gray and blue, floaters dragging their amoebic way across what should have been my field of vision.

"He's no doppelgänger, Gem."

"Well, duh." Olivia squeezed my hand, then let it go. "Told you it's Tony."

"Yes, that's kind of obvious now." Gemma's throaty chuckle carried more nerves than humor. "But how in the name of the king is he not dead?"

"Supposedly," I blinked, hoping that'd make the remnants of temporary blinding go away faster, "I've got nine lives."

"Wow, mister." The kid's voice was unmistakably higher-pitched than her mom's, with a completely different timbre and tone. She sounded like her father. "Are you a Kells Cat?"

"There's no such thing anymore." I crossed my arms over my chest. "Everybody knows that the whole point of a Kells Cat is to deliver decrees that the monarchs make together. That saying about killing the messenger is the reason they get nine lives. And since we have divorced monarchs, they ain't making joint decrees." I wasn't going to tell the kid about how they'd gotten wiped out during the multiple genocides in the early twentieth century. "Anyway, they're fairy tales, kid."

"I think it's more likely some kind of Undeath Magus gave you some help when you were too young to remember." Admiral Tolland stroked his beard and squinted at me. "You've lived under a dangerous roof." He smirked. "Kid."

"Yeah, probably more likely." I sighed, somehow relieved that he'd gotten off the subject. I knew enough about Undeath magic to understand I wasn't affected by it, though.

"Well, wait a minute." Olivia's voice turned my head. "The queen has a suitor. Doesn't that mean the Under will need a Kells Cat eventually? If she accepts, I mean. There might be some joint decrees, then."

"That's not something I want to think about." Gemma, the formidable-looking Unseelie troll pirate captain, shuddered. "You saw him trying to blast those waterlogged vampires out of the water at midsummer. He's not the kind of monarch the Under needs."

"But could he ever actually be king, anyway?"

"If he knocks the queen up, his kid could be." I shook my head, then glanced at the wide-eyed kid. "Oops, sorry. Not really appropriate topic with a preschooler around."

"I'm five!" The kid stuck her tongue out and blew a raspberry at me. "And I know where babies come from."

She was an odd little thing, all pale skin like her dad with that orange hair. Something about her birdlike build reminded me of Olivia, but that made no sense at all, considering her parentage. I glanced at Olivia. Her skin was the same color as the kid's, her hair almost light enough for her to be a Sidhe changeling. But changelings couldn't be shifters. My whiskers twinged.

"Well, still." I shrugged. "Anyway, it's possible is all I'm saying. Also, she could give him the rank of prince, which would let him challenge either monarch. But she wouldn't go and do something that risky."

"But both of those scenarios are possible," said Gemma. "It's healthy to worry about either happening."

"Listen here," The Admiral put his hands on his hips, looming so large that he dwarfed just about everything else in the small cabin. "You kids have done this on your own long enough. This Hopewell rascal's got more power than everyone in your pack combined and decades more experience to boot. Even Duke Ismail hasn't got as many active years under his belt. You need bigger guns on your side of this battle, or you'll get yourselves sunk."

"That's true." Olivia gave me a sidelong glance. "And I've said as much over and over. But you'll have to take that up with Josh. He calls those shots because he's the Alpha."

"I don't need permission from a half-grown puppy." Admiral Tolland's chest puffed up like a toad's. If toads were the size of professional wrestlers and had tusks, the resemblance would be perfect. "It's time Hopewell's elders and betters began applying boot to bottom, and I aim to do just that."

"That's true." Gemma smiled. "I think it's time you Tinfoil Hat folks had some allies to help you flank and corner this Extramagus."

"I couldn't have put that better myself." The voice was way too recently familiar.

"Oh, no." I shook my head, not wanting to turn around and confirm the source of the voice behind me. "Not my disappearing-reappearing-godmother again."

"Hello, Tony." Kiki stepped lightly across the floor, nimbly dodging blades that flowered from the cuffs of Admiral Tolland's sleeves and a shot from Gemma's pistol. "I'd apologize for making myself scarce earlier, but I'm not sorry. And I wouldn't be here now if you'd gotten more of a move on earlier."

She stopped next to Olivia. "Oh, you're just perfect. I mean that with absolute sincerity. I haven't seen such a brilliant owlish specimen since—" She chuckled. "Tch. I've gotten ahead of myself again, and we don't have time. Or you don't. You'll be late to meet the king if you don't set sail in the next five minutes."

"Hoist sail, and set course to the Midnight Cape." Gemma clapped her hands, and I heard the slapping of invisible webbed feet. She locked eyes with her grandfather. "One of us should be up there to supervise, or those sea nymphs will sail us to the other end of the map from where we need to be just for kicks."

"Aye." Admiral Tolland set the kid on his shoulders. "Come along, Hope."

I watched them go. When I turned around to see what else Kiki might have wanted, she was in the middle of swiping one of the kid's drawings from a footlocker.

"Wow, your godmother's a real piece of work, Tony," said Gemma. "I mean, who steals stuff from kids?"

"Ladies, apparently. Kitsune get bored in the Under, I guess."

"Okay. This is officially the third strangest day of my entire life." Gemma strode to the door and shut it with a decisive clomp. "None of you are going anywhere until you give me the whole story of how you got in the Under and how you all managed to be in half-shifted forms."

"It's a long stor—"

"No time to expl—"

Gemma clapped her hands again, cutting us both off. "You've got twenty minutes. Spill it or walk the plank. Legal Owl can start, and I'll hear from Hinky cat-man after that. Extinct nobility brings up the rear."

Olivia and I sang like freaking canaries. My godmother, not so much.

CHAPTER ELEVEN

Olivia

I told Gemma everything I knew, which didn't seem like much. A few times, I caught glimpses of Tony from the corner of my eye. His face alternated between a strained sort of pallor and crimson with eyes unable to rise above floor view level. When I finished, I'd intended to focus on his story, try to absorb everything he said. His godmother had other plans.

"So, you're the Ga— Um." The lady cleared her throat. "The gal Tony adores."

"I'd hardly say that Miss—" I turned my head in her direction, craning it in a more unnatural way than was strictly necessary. "I'm sorry, but I don't believe we've been formally introduced."

"It's Kiki, no need for a Lady or a Miss." Her smile reminded me of Josh Dennison's. Canine for sure.

"Thanks, Kiki." I grinned back at her, trying to remind myself not to let my guard down around this mysterious woman. But I failed at not staring, knowing that the scarf on her head concealed fox ears. I couldn't help myself, had to ask without actually phrasing a question. "So, you're partially shifted, too."

"It's not her turn to talk." Gemma stepped up beside the Kitsune, tapping one booted foot on the floor. "But I have to admit, the fact that you literally popped in and haven't popped out again has me curious. So I'm changing up the order for now. Tell us why you're here, Kiki."

"Oh, for the same reason most of us are here, of course." The left corner of her mouth tilted up. "Our parents got together at some point, we were born. And then, we got some trinkets that made us special. Well, more so than the usual Extrahuman at any rate."

"Trinkets?" Tony's eyebrows tried to meet his hairline. "I don't remember getting anything like that."

"Well, you wouldn't." Kiki's grin showed too many teeth for a genuine smile. Her ears drooped a bit, something I'd seen before on dismayed wolf shifters. "I was there when you got yours, Tony. And you, Olivia."

"Don't tell me I'm part of the trinket club, too." Gemma put her hands on her hips.

"Nope." Kiki shook her head. "But I am." She pulled the sash from around her waist, revealing all of her tails. "Of course, I got mine ages before either of you."

"You'll tell us how people get these trinkets," said Gemma. "Now."

"The person who gets one must have compatible magical potential." Kiki gazed at Tony. "You can't become a magical cat shifter unless you're already going to be a cat shifter, for example."

"There must be more to it than that." I scratched my head.

"Yes." Kiki shut her eyes, squeezing the lids together tightly like a child afraid of the dark. "The person must be born in the Under. And finally, the original bearer must have the trinket cut off or out of their body before a new person can get it."

"Hoo, boy." I watched Kiki's tails waving from behind her in counterpoint, unable to tell whether there were eight or nine of them now. Insight struck me like a splash of cold water. "That's got something to do with why Tony ended up in the Under."

"Also with why the king picked you for a Quest, Olivia." Gemma pointed at my wings. "He must have known you'd be like this when you came here."

"That makes sense." I nodded. "I'd have been pretty useless at apprehending a fugitive as a little owl."

"We still don't know who he means." Gemma caught my eye, then jerked her chin at Kiki.

"No." Tony shook his head and crossed his arms over his chest. "I ain't handing my godmother over to nobody. I'd be dead for good if it weren't for her."

"Well, I'd be surprised by that." Kiki tittered from behind her fingers. "The Goblin King's seen me before at his court, and he's never acted as though I shouldn't be there. I didn't get the title of lady from a Crackerjack box."

"Masked balls don't count, Kiki." Gemma waggled one pink, sparkly fingernail at the Kitsune.

"That's not all I've been to, you know." Kiki winked. She belonged in a Lewis Carrol novel, and I wasn't sure whether or not that meant I liked her.

"'*I do live in a topsy-turvy world,*'" I quoted.

"Yes!" Kiki tapped the end of her nose with one finger. "'It seems I have to do something wrong first, in order to learn from that what not to do!'"

"She knows *Alice in Wonderland*," Tony ticked off each title on one hand as he spoke. "Tolkien, and fortune cookies, but jack and squat about anything important."

"That's not the way nice young men are supposed to speak to their godmother," said Kiki, "but I suppose nice is different from good, so you're not exactly one of those."

"Stop deflecting and finish your story, Kitsune." Gemma's hand hovered over the butt of her pistol.

"Oh, very well." Kiki raised an eyebrow at Gemma. "I'm not

the one who derailed us, but that's neither here nor there. I'm sure you'd like to know the reason I've been here in the Under all this time in the first place."

"Everyone does." I nodded.

"It's far more complicated than I can explain for now." Kiki sighed and shook her head. "I've been reclaiming some items of extreme importance for the continuation of my species."

"So, you're stealing?" Gemma's hand dropped closer to her weapon.

"Reclaiming." Bushy red-orange and white tails peeked out again from under Kiki's sash. "No creature has any real use for Kitsune tails except for my kin and me."

"You don't have any kin," said Tony. "Well, not technically, because we're not related."

"Wrong on the former and right on the latter." Kiki reached under the scarf on her head to scratch an ear. "Too itchy. Ugh."

"Wait!" I clapped my hands to match the ideas going off like fireworks in my brain. "The tails are trinkets, like the ones you say Tony and I have!"

"In a sense, although they are different in some intricate ways I don't have time to mention." Kiki grinned. "You grew up much sharper than your parents were, Olivia."

"This is the second time someone's mentioned my birth parents as though they're dead." I shivered. "It's giving me the creeps."

"I'm sorry." Kiki closed her eyes. "It's not my place to talk about that."

I stood blinking at the Kitsune, wondering what her words and change of mood might mean. There weren't any more fireworks left in the night sky of my head, the space too clouded with the smoky aftermath of implications about magical shifters.

Something warm and soft brushed against my hand, then curled around my wrist. I looked down to see a dark-furred appendage twining around my arm and then my hand. Tony had his back to me, his body obscuring half of mine from the others in a posture I recognized as protective. I blinked one last time, then sighed, trying to contain the combination of bewilderment and hope racing through my veins. Tony Gitano was holding my hand.

"Look, I still need to hear from Tony, anyway." Gemma cleared her throat. "About how he's still alive."

But as it turned out, that tale wasn't Tony's to tell.

Tony

"You know, that's something I'd like to hear more about, too." I tried not to hiss after completing the sentence. That sort of thing came with a tail gesture I didn't want to make. My tail was happy right where it was on Olivia's wrist, thank you very much. "Kiki was with me when I woke up in the woods between the beach and a Gnomehill. I still don't know how I got there."

"Hmm," said Gemma. "I bet it's because she said she didn't have time to tell you or something like that."

"Exactamundo." I nodded. "So, spill the beans, Godmother."

"I arranged for that." Kiki laced her hands together in front of her, the balls of her thumbs pressed together like they were praying even if she wasn't. "A Gnome named Gee owed me a favor, and they paid it by getting you out of the morgue and into the Under. I gave them a Foxfire-infused trinket to help him cover his tracks."

"But Gee-Nome was with Bianca." Olivia gave my godmother the stink-eye. "She confirmed the alibi and everything."

"You forgetting something important about Gnomes, Olivia." I sighed. "They bend time. It's plausible."

"I'm glad you feel that way because it's the only thing I can tell you." Kiki nodded.

"But wait." I flicked my ears, annoyed at myself for being a moron. "Vanishing works on any living creature to transport them anywhere, but it only gets a dead one to either the place they died or where they were born."

"So that's got to be what happened." Kiki looked me right in the eye. "You died in Olneyville, and that's not where you ended up."

"Hoo, boy!" Olivia shook my tail off her hand, then smacked her forehead. "So Hope was right. Maybe you really are a Kells Cat, Tony. I knew it. Professor Watkins mentioned that you were born in the Under. Some other shifter, too."

Kiki put her hands over her mouth and let out a cough that sounded like a word.

"Say that again."

"I said, 'you.'" My godmother couldn't meet Olivia's eyes. "This is your birthplace, too." She yelped, then pressed her palms to her temples. "I can't tell you any more. I already said it's not my place."

"Oh." Gemma peered at Kiki's grimacing face. "She's under a ban to prevent her from talking about it or something. Powerful stuff." Gemma didn't say what we all knew. A ban that strong was more than a Gnome could cook up.

"Yes." She nodded. "I couldn't have my mind wiped, not with the reclaiming I still needed to do. A ban was the only other option."

"Okay, so let me get this straight." Gemma held up one fist, raising a finger for each item on her list. "Tony actually died. He's a magic shifter because of some kind of trinket. Olivia's also a magic trinket creature. They were both born in the Under. Kiki is here to collect tails. Tell me if I'm missing anything."

"I believe that's it, Captain Tolland." Kiki nodded. The twinkle had come back to her eyes. I wrinkled my nose at the feeling of relief that rode in with it.

"But I bet you can't tell us anything useful, like exactly what kinds of magical shifters we are." I chewed my lower lip, wishing I dared ask my godmother a direct question.

"Hmm." Her smile showed more teeth than I'd have thought possible. "No, I can't confirm or deny any guesses made earlier. All I can say is that you are a special sort, Tony, and Olivia, extraordinarily so."

"Flattery doesn't work on me." I caught Olivia's skeptical stare from the corner of my eye.

"That's good because it shouldn't." Kiki nodded. "I want you to be on your worst behavior but best judgment while you're here, and also immediately after you get out of the Faerie realm."

"This from the woman who lectured me on manners earlier today." I rolled my eyes.

"Yes." She clapped her hands. "This is the king's demesne. It's contradictory by nature and dangerous if you don't pay attention. Unexpected elements show up as a matter of course. Olivia, you must put your foot down when instinct tells you to. It's the only way to complete the Quest His Majesty's put you on. I've got some advice for you too, Tony."

"Lay it on me."

"You've got a chance to claw some of your lives back if you play to your greatest strength," she said, "but it's slim. You'll need help. And you ought to try." Kiki looked from Olivia to Gemma and back. She put one hand on the side of her mouth and lowered her voice. "He's only got one left right now."

"Great." I rolled my eyes. "Awesome." I turned my head to look at Gemma and Olivia. "Thanks for telling everyone in the universe." I flapped a hand to the side to emphasize my sarcasm. "What am I supposed to do about it, anyway?"

But Kiki had vanished. The footlocker stood open.

"Great." I stood midway between Olivia and Gemma, hands on my hips. "Exactly what I need. A disappearing-reappearing light-fingered godmother."

"We've got enough to do without worrying about Kiki."

Gemma strode toward the cabin's door. "It's almost time to dock and drop anchor."

"Well, color me worried." I sighed. "Kitsunes aren't supposed to be able to vanish themselves. Kiki had help. This time, it definitely couldn't have been Gee-Nome, who's recuperating in the Gnomehill. I wonder if Kiki's agenda really is just chasing tails."

"Protecting you, maybe?" Olivia shrugged. "I mean, she's your godmother, so she must have been important to your mom, right?"

"Dunno. I don't remember meeting anyone like her." I shook my head, absolutely stumped. "Besides, she told me she's been in the Under for ages. Then again, I was born here, so…" I shrugged.

"That's a mystery for now, then." Gemma pushed the door open. "I bet the king knows something."

"Yeah." Olivia stood up, then headed for the door. "We don't want to keep Ron waiting."

"Wow." Gemma stood there, blinking. "Olivia Adler's moving up in the Extrahuman world."

"He told me to call him that because of the whole Quest thing." She shrugged, passing Gemma as she went out the door. "Nothing else to it besides that."

"Better not be." My words came out more like a growl than anything else. I fought the urge to cover my mouth. After that, I bit my lip to keep from screaming in frustration. I'd hesitated with Olivia, made her wait because everything was so dangerous. And now the Goblin King himself wanted to put the moves on her? I couldn't blame him, but it made my blood boil all the same.

"Down, boy." Gemma snorted. "That's not what I meant." I heard the door close behind us and then Gemma strode forward, passing me and then Olivia. After that, she turned around and walked backward. "Look, you're obviously some kind of faerie creature, judging by the whole three questions business we went through earlier."

"So, I'm like a Sidhe or something?"

"Maybe, maybe not." Gemma stared hard at Olivia's hair. "It's just a theory. I really don't know."

"I think so, too." I paced slowly, remaining behind Olivia. "But Olivia getting favors hasn't worked on me. This whole set of shenanigans might be a ploy to get her into debt on the Unseelie side."

"I can't believe you're telling me all this." Gemma grinned. "I mean, I owe Olivia a favor, and somehow, you're both spilling your guts to me."

"You're the captain, Gemma." Olivia chuckled. "Besides, I'm a stranger in a strange land here. So I'll need all the help I can get. And I don't expect anyone to give me a hand if they don't even know what I'm doing in the first place."

"I hope I'm wrong." My tail flicked from side to side, no matter what I did to stop the traitor appendage from giving all of my feelings away. "You're way too honest to be a faerie anything. Kiki knows everything about what you are but can't say. I don't think you're a changeling. You don't smell like one, for one thing."

"Oh, and what does she smell like then, Tony?" Gemma waggled her eyebrows, her grin goofier than a vaudeville performer's.

"Heaven." I cleared my throat. Had I meant to say that? My face felt like it'd just been slapped by a giant-sized palm.

"Nice!" Gemma held one fist up. I sighed and rolled my eyes, but she didn't put it down. I tapped it with mine.

"Hey!" Olivia rolled her eyes. "I'm right here with you guys, you know?"

"Yeah, I know." I stopped walking and stuck my tail out, blocking her path. I figured at that point, it was now or never. She had the king's attention, but so far, he hadn't asked anything of her but a Quest. Maybe I wouldn't be too late if only I could say what needed saying now. "And it's about time I told you—"

My voice was drowned in a wall of sound. A low, throbbing,

howl besieged my ears, leaving behind a rubble of ringing when it stopped. That was why I saw the king before I heard his boots hit the planking on the dock we'd moored at. Instead of the ragged black tuxedo, he wore a softly draped cloak over a doublet and hose. Olivia blinked a few times, looking like she used to at high noon on all her meds. He'd dazzled her, of course. He was the king, after all.

"Where does he get off, anyway?" I grumbled. "Matching his clothes to your feathers is just tacky."

"Actually, it's technically the opposite, young Mr. Gitano." The king inclined his head toward me. "I'm glad to see with my own eyes that you walk among the living again, and that you've decided to aid my champion. I will need to steal her away for the moment, however."

And just like that, I had to let her go.

CHAPTER TWELVE

Olivia

Ron stretched one of his hands out toward me, tenting his hand in the same way he had back at Swan Point Cemetery. Even with the familiar gesture, I could tell he was not strictly the same creature I'd met before. Here in the Under, the Goblin King would brook no insult, offer no indulgence. I adjusted my address accordingly.

"You didn't tell me I was a champion, Your Majesty." I held my hand under his since he seemed to expect it, and I wasn't about to piss the king off in his own demesne, even if he'd called me here. My shoulders tightened, a symptom of my efforts not to turn my head around to look at Tony. My life was weirder than ever, walking with the king of all things Unseelie while pining over a cat straight out of Schrödinger's theorem.

"You weren't quite that at the time." The king paced down the dock, and I went with him on my own feet this time. I'd gotten less clumsy on land since my wings had decided to put in an appearance. He seemed to realize that, too, knew it without having to be told. Instead of warm and fuzzy, the whole thing felt uncannily ticklish, like a spider walking on my neck. "You are now, however."

"Okay, then. Champion it is." I grinned and glanced up at him. His eyes looked soft and fond, alight with a sort of affection. It reminded me of the way some people look at their pets. "Hopefully, I made it here on time."

"Yes." The king's eyes tilted down and behind me for a moment. When they returned to mine, he shook his head. "And I see you've found my Garters."

"I suppose you want them back." I clapped my free hand over my mouth. Not only did I sound like Captain Obvious, but I'd also engaged in banter. Bantering with faerie royalty hadn't been my intention. If the queen was anything like the king, I had no idea how Richard Hopewell handled being near her. A healthy dose of Narcissistic Personality Disorder, maybe. It'd take something like that to feel more than halfway significant beside a Faerie monarch. And I'd just sassed off to one by some error of instinct. "Um. Sorry to presume."

"No need to apologize. You suppose correctly." He sighed. "But I can't have them now. The Garters choose who wields them, for good or ill. I've had my day. You're the one this time around. And you'll need them, for your Quest and perhaps beyond."

"You said you'd give me the particulars on that." In the silence that followed my statement, I heard Tony mutter something behind us. The fire returned to my belly. He'd been about to tell me something important. It wasn't as bad as wondering whether he was dead, but I swallowed my anger over Tony walking behind me, fuming. He followed at a distance which respected the king's wishes but made it clear that he wasn't happy about it.

"You and your party must be adequately equipped for the coming chase." He turned his head, gazing up at a chalet on the cliff overlooking the sea. The king's brow creased, and for a scant span of seconds, he looked elderly. When he turned back to face me, the smile he wore would have looked at home on the face of an elementary-schooler. He snapped his fingers. "Done."

"What to the who now?" A gale came in over the water, but only my shoulders felt cold. Tony let out a low whistle. I looked down.

Instead of a tattered old beach dress, a skirt of feathers matching my wings covered me from the waist down. A sleeveless doublet of blue leather covered my torso, molded perfectly to my form. It left my arms free for drawing a bow and loosing arrows.

Instead of flip-flops, moccasin-style boots covered my feet and calves. The right one sported a sheath with a boot dagger. I tugged at the hilt and it came free, revealing a silver blade with copper edging.

"That's sick!" Tony strode forward to peer at my new weapon. "Sick and twisted. What did he say we're fighting?"

"He didn't, yet." I looked back up at the king, hoping whatever expectant expression my face wore wouldn't offend him.

"He'll tell you soon." The Goblin King smirked, reminding me of the time he'd popped in at Josh's to give Ismail an unexpected promotion. He seemed ageless and all ages at the same time, mercurial. I wondered how much of a headache that gave him.

"Will His Majesty give me some swag, too?" Tony raised an eyebrow, crossing his arms over his chest. "I'm helping your champion, after all."

"How...hmm, appropriate." The king's smirk vanished, his flinty eyes losing any warmth they'd held. "It's been nearly a century since one of your kind walked the Under, and ages since one allied with a creature like my current champion."

"Enough with the cryptic statements, Majesty." Tony's mouth puckered around the honorific as though it were a lime. "If you're in the mood to hand out gear, make with the gifting already. Payment's part of even your flexible rules."

Tony

I stood facing the king, tapping my foot in time with my flicking tail. I didn't give two shakes that he was a Faerie monarch. If he needed help so badly, he'd have to pay somehow. I didn't owe him jack or squat, and I wasn't about to let him imply that I did.

"Ah," said the king. "I would, but it seems that you are already reasonably prepared."

"But I ain't a Boy Scout, and everybody knows it, so don't mock me, Your Majesty." I knew my way around faerie everything. All the same, Olivia blinked at me like I'd just made a faux pas instead of using a sound negotiating tactic. "I ain't prepared for a magical owl shifter's Quest. You want her to have the best chance at success, you want to make sure her help has similar odds."

"You talk sense, young Mister Gitano." The king snapped his fingers. "There." He waved a hand at my shoulders. They itched a little.

"Huh." I reached up with both hands, not sure what to expect. Two buttons now hung from my epaulets, one silver, and the other copper. The storm flap on my coat felt heavy. I reached under it to find it reinforced with chain mail. I patted my rain guard, which had the same upgrade. The itching got worse somehow, and deeper. It felt like the muscles between my shoulders had itching powder all over them, but I couldn't call the king out for a prank at that point. I also couldn't complain about only getting some armor and a couple of lousy buttons. "Thanks, Your Majesty."

The king only smiled. I didn't mind that much until he turned the expression toward Olivia and it widened. I almost didn't blame him, she had that same effect on me. But she was the only person who made me feel like smiling more. The Goblin King could find some other bird to coax onto his perch. He leaned over and whispered something in her ear.

I should have overheard the whole thing but only managed to catch a bit. After the king put his arm around her shoulders, the only sound was my blood pounding with jealousy. The itching on my back gave me an idea of what it must be like to have rabies. I was on the verge of pitching some mad fit, my ears flattening against my head. Before I could hiss, he stepped off, leaving Olivia's face a tangle of eyebrows and chewed lower lip.

"Now that you've had your briefing, get to the summit and begin tracking the interloper. My hunting party will follow at a distance. I expect great things from both of you." The king put his right hand over his head like he wanted someone to give him five. He clapped his own left hand against it and vanished.

"Great." I stared at the cliff ahead of us, stumped by the path snaking up its side. At least that blasted itching had finally stopped. "Maybe you should go without me, after all." My tail twitched even though I'd tried to stop it. I hated how everyone could tell when I was angry or scared because of the stupid tail. And from where I stood, His Royal Majesty was friendlier with Olivia than I liked. Then again, it didn't matter what I liked. Someone else's opinion on the matter was more important, of course. I held my tongue, waiting for her to weigh in. "Maybe the king doesn't want me around."

"I don't care what he thinks. I need you." Her big amber eyes scanned the trees near the top of the path, stopping at a shadowy spot on the farther side. "Come on, Tony. Let's go."

"There's no way we'll climb that anytime soon." I shook my head and crossed my arms over my chest. My coat felt too tight.

"Um, Tony?" Olivia stretched her wings and shook them a little. "With a pair of these, you can get just about anywhere." She flapped her wings once, then looked at me. No, her gaze was fixed over my shoulder again.

I tried to look at whatever she saw without turning around, but I couldn't because I wasn't an owl shifter with a neck right out of *The Exorcist*. The itching and the tightness in my trench coat gave me some of the craziest suspicions. I moved my arms, about to shrug off my coat and leave myself vulnerable.

"Wait." Olivia walked behind me. Her presence there made me burn with the most inappropriate sense of anticipation. I just knew she was about to touch me, and waiting for that had me twitchier than being in a room full of rocking chairs. I wasn't exactly happy about it, either. There's no time for romance or even flat-out lust when you've got to track quarry ahead of an Unseelie Hunt.

I felt a gust of air as Olivia unbuttoned the tab holding my coat's back vent closed, then she tugged on the belt. I shook like a skyscraper in an earthquake, couldn't help it. When her fingertips brushed what strained against the heavy fabric, I noticed that she trembled, too. I closed my eyes, the back of my eyelids replaying that afternoon when she'd kissed me in the shadow of the Dennisons' wall. I'd felt like I could fly that day, until the reality of how I'd put Olivia in danger if I claimed her as mine crashed my hopes worse than Icarus. A breeze blew down the hillside, twinging my whiskers and ruffling my feathers.

"Feathers?"

"Yes, Tony." I opened my eyes to see Olivia standing in front of me. "The king gave you wings. I adjusted your coat to let them out. Try them." A smile tugged the corners of her mouth. I flexed the muscles in my back, kicking up a gust behind me. "Hoo, boy."

"Hoo, girl." My own face twisted as I tried not to laugh.

She did, and I lost it.

That laughter was like the time I went to a cathartic screaming therapy session, only a million times better. Our faces stretched and streaked with tears. When she dabbed her eyes and I screwed my fists under mine, we were ready to discuss the important stuff.

"I don't know how to fly."

"Don't worry, it'll be fun. The king said it'd come naturally to you because of what you are." I could have launched into a list of questions about that, but we had just as much time for that as declarations of affection or whatever.

"So this Quest is gonna be a piece of cake, huh?" I winked. "Lead on."

"Cake in a cup." Olivia pointed up the headache-inducing path. "Come on, then. Let's fly!" She held out her arm like some old-timey lady going on a stroll.

If it'd been anyone but her, I'd have turned tail and headed anywhere else, but I couldn't let her go alone. It's dangerous to do that. Anyway, I might as well have stayed dead if I wasn't going to help Olivia. I didn't take her arm, though. It would have been lame for her, linking arms with me after touching freaking royalty. I closed my eyes, trying not to remember how her lips had felt during that one brief shining moment they'd been pressed to mine six months earlier. How could I burn with fiery green jealousy over a woman I didn't deserve? Bah humbug.

"Fine," I said. The lie left a flat and sour taste in my mouth.

"Copy me like I'm Lynn Frampton and this is a science exam." She walked ahead of me, her shoulders tilted further down than I'd seen them since the moment before she'd turned around to see I was really alive back in the Gnomehill. She had to feel pretty low for me to notice that with her wings open.

I went back to the patented Tony Gitano pastime of kicking myself. Right before the king showed up, I'd been about to tell Olivia in no uncertain terms how important she was to me even if those damn torpedoes weren't love, exactly. Now I wasn't so sure a declaration from one lame cat shifter would matter. After all, every time my feelings had mattered before, they'd gotten me into trouble.

Tilting my wings forward, I raced in Olivia's wake. The air she'd displaced played with my new feathers. She reminded me less of a celestial being now, although that idea had never strayed far when she was around. If she was like an angel, then I was a soul condemned to Hell, and my own father was my jailer.

Dad had always tried to suss me out, discover whether I cared about things, and then turn them on me like daggers. It was a strange kind of torture, designed to get something other than information out of me. My emotions were his ammo the handful of times we got into a moral shootout. I wasn't innocent either because it's hard not to copy the person who's supposed to know better. Feelings were landmines on the Gitano Family battlefield. Stepping on the wrong one proved deadly.

The air and our speed lifted us. I floundered, pulled more than I expected by the wind's currents. As we took to the half-lit skies, I spied the king's hunting lodge off to my right. The lower light gave everything a black, white, and ruddy cast.

It turned out that flying was easy. Olivia swayed before me, flapping to gain more altitude. I mirrored her movements, my wings carrying me without the strain I expected. Soon, I paced her. I set my mind free to wander. A month earlier, I'd stood in Josh Dennison's basement, breaking stuff and making noise about how Dick Hopewell the Extramagus could just bring it. I'd been so focused on the big bad, I'd forgotten about the near and constant threat of dear old Dad in my life. That had given him the opportunity to kill me.

"Why did you bother bringing me along, anyway?" I shut my trap too late. Flying wasn't an autopilot proposition, after all. At least, I thought, she wouldn't be able to hear me in all the wind. But the king had fixed it so she could, somehow.

Olivia

"What kind of question is that, Tony?"

"The lame kind, I guess." He snorted. "Shouldn't have asked it."

"There's no such thing as a stupid question."

"Of course, you quote Watkins at a time like this."

"That's not Watkins, it's you." My wings fluttered, which

wasn't ideal with the downdrafts. "Watch out up here—turbulence. My bad."

"Okay." Tony's tail twisted out behind him, probably helping him navigate the gusty mess I'd made. "And I don't remember saying anything like that."

"You don't remember the first day we met?"

"Yeah, I remember." He clammed up after that. My throat tightened with the idea that he'd forgotten it all.

There was no way I'd ever forget that early autumn day, the sun too bright even for my medicated eyes. Tony had looked like an oasis of black, absorbing the light. I was drawn to him like some kind of reverse moth to a dark flame. I'd tugged his sleeve without thinking. The way he'd flinched struck my heart like an arrow to the chest. So I'd stopped breathing, thought my heart stopped, too.

I only wanted to ask directions, hadn't intended to look into his face. And there I found a portrait of terror like he'd been expecting someone else. And then he'd smiled. All that fear melted away, leaving behind an obstinate allure. I gasped, realizing that here was a man who'd never give up. And then I yawned like an idiot. He laughed, not at me but with me. More like we were in on some secret joke together.

"Earth to Tony."

"Yeah, okay." He cleared his throat. "You asked me if I knew where the magic school was like you thought I was just a regular guy and not a crime lord's kid."

"I did. And then I apologized for asking such a stupid question. And that's when you said—"

"Ain't no such thing as a stupid question." Tony chuckled, not the reaction I'd expected.

Remembering the first time we met had me close to tears for some reason, as though it was something dead and buried. Angry tears, of course. Not at Tony, either. If he had trouble remembering, it had something to do with being mostly dead for a week. I swallowed it all, letting the wind flash-dry the remains of my near-crying experience.

"And do you remember what happened after that?" I banked, wheeling around as I saw the hunting party. I went on ahead of them, due southeast. The interloper had gone that way, according to the moon-tinted energy trail he'd left behind.

"Yeah." Tony banked, too, flapping to catch up before speaking again. "You started asking me the weirdest questions you could think of."

"Can a refrigerator enter the Boston Marathon?" I let my voice travel back in time to that sunlit day, trying to recapture the lost moments.

"Can a spider web catch a cold?" Tony chuckled.

"Does butter fly?" I glanced at him, only to find him staring at me.

"Okay, I get it." He looked away. "So the question isn't stupid. So answer it, maybe. Why me and not a troll with rank who happens to owe you a big favor?"

"Don't get me wrong, Gemma's a good person and all, but I like having you around, Tony." I brushed my hair back over my shoulder and turned to look again at him. Our eyes met like the divide between the light and dark sides of the moon.

"Well, nobody's perfect." He didn't blink, even with the wind.

"Oh, Tony." This time, I broke our gazes. Good thing, too. "Look, someone's down there."

We banked, landing on the peak of an oddly pointed hill. I bounded down the hill's south side, arrow nocked. At the bottom, no one was there. I turned, intending to call Tony off, and saw the door. I pointed, showing Tony the heavy chain and locks barring our entry. He jerked his chin at the ground, which offered up a set of footprints, canine and heavy enough for the creature we sought. They disappeared under the door.

"Can you get in?"

"You're kidding, right?" He smirked. "People with paws can't pick locks."

"Look at it again, though." I leaned over, casting a shadow over the mechanism.

"Huh." Tony squinted. "Looks like it's four legs good, two legs bad as far as this door's concerned."

"*Animal Farm*?" I rolled my eyes. "At a time like this? Can you open it or not?"

"Yeah, this is why everybody loves me." Tony squatted to get a look at the latch. "My breaking-and-entering skills are so desirable, they cause throngs of people to weep and fall at my feet. I'm a regular robbery rock star." He rolled his eyes.

"Hoo, boy," I said after I stopped giggling. "We're not breaking and entering. The king's sent us on a Quest, and this is still his demesne."

"Well, this thing ain't budging." Tony stood up. "At least, not with mundane effort."

"What'll we do?"

"Don't worry, I've got something up my sleeve." He tucked his right hand in, then pulled something out of his coat, leaving the trench half dangling off his back. I giggled.

"Literally!" Both my hands covered my mouth. "Sorry."

CHAPTER THIRTEEN

Tony

"No, don't." Before I could stop and think, my left hand shot out and grasped her wrist. "Don't cover your laughter. Don't apologize for it."

"Okay." Olivia lowered her hands, turned them, and held them in front of her, palms out. She looked me right in the eye and said, "Sorry."

I laughed so hard my whole body did a shuck and jive. I stepped on the tail of my trench coat, slipped, and went ass over elbows into the door. It opened, and I fell across its threshold, just barely managing to keep hold of the magipyschic lockpicking tools in my right hand. I gazed up at Olivia, momentarily stunned like a mouse at midnight.

Olivia Adler made everything all right. Her wide-eyed eureka moments, the way she masked high humor with deadpan. Her very presence put me at ease. As a partner in any venture, the owl shifter was second to none. She only used her powers for good, never letting her anger hurt anyone but herself, tears its only outlet. I knew she cared about me, but if there was a time and place for us, this wasn't it. I'd wait forever for her.

Flopping on flagstones, I swung my arm out behind me in an attempt to grab the loose sleeve of my trench coat. I felt naked without its comforting weight around both of my shoulders. With that thought, I stopped moving and took a deep breath.

"Hey, Olivia?"

"Yeah?"

"If I got vanished in the middle of my autopsy, why do I have my trench coat and all its tricks?"

"Hoo, boy." She crinkled up her forehead. "I don't know. I bet Kiki does, though."

"Yeah, maybe." I shook my head. "That doesn't feel right. Dunno why. Could be because Gnomes don't think much about mortal things like wanting our particular clothes."

"I agree about Kiki not acting on her own to get you here." Olivia reached a hand down and I took it, letting go as soon as I got up. Clammy hands, *no bene*. Her grip lingered, though, implying that she didn't seem to mind.

"Well, okay. So you think good old Godmom knows more about who did than she's telling, then?"

"Yeah. She has to know, has to be covering for whoever ordered it." She scratched her head. "It makes no sense, though. I mean, why?"

"You're a bit new to the whole faerie favors thing. It makes sense to me, and here's why." I took a deep breath, counting to five. Then, I let it out, not bothering with the numbers. I was past that, at least over the matter of Kiki and her fake-outs. "There had to be a favor involved to get me into the Under. Whoever owed it, that's who gave the orders, made the arrangements."

"But why hide it, then?" Olivia shook her head that hair of hers tumbling all around her face. I clasped my hands behind my back to keep from reaching out to stroke it.

"The person who owed her has got to be extremely high on

the food chain here." I looked out the door, up at the eternally twilit sky.

"Ismail?"

"Dukes are small fish." I shook my head. "Besides, djinn can't vanish people without being bound to a lamp."

"Oh, Tony." Olivia's eyes were like twin moons. "I know who it was. The one who's let Kiki stay here all this time, as though it's a privilege owed to her. R—"

"No." I held one finger to her lips. "Don't say any of his names. If he wants this secret kept, we have got to respect it."

"Okay." She blinked, then reached up and took my hand. "I just wish I knew why."

"Simple." I sighed, trying to ease out of her grasp. "He needs me here, helping you. Shoulda known."

"I'll take it." She squeezed my hand. "For now. And only because we have a wolf shifter to track."

I froze. "The interloper's not Kiki?"

"No." She shook her head and started off down the darkened corridor. "I'm not sure who he is, but he's been in here without permission since spring."

"Interesting." Our footsteps echoed, mingling in ways I told my imagination to stop extrapolating. My fear for my godmother melted away.

"How so?"

"Some Feds came to Rhode Island back in the spring, after the whole Dennison pack business and before that drive-by on Blaine, Kim, and Jeannie."

"Did they get an anonymous tip or something?"

"Not so anonymous, actually." I glanced her way, saw her nod. "I overheard Dad mention helping with procuring something to take out a Harcourt or few."

"We know that didn't go so well for him, thank goodness."

"Yeah, but that's not entirely the point. One of the Feds was a Psychic, Special Agent Natalie something. She's the one who ordered a Summoner to put a brownie pretending to be home decor in there. Her partner was a wolf shifter. He went missing before Blaine buried his stepdad."

"Hoo, boy." Olivia paused, tilting her head. "I think we're getting close."

"Yeah, hush time." I made a gesture like a zipper over my lips, and she nodded.

I stepped more carefully, trying to mask my footfalls. Olivia copied me, and it worked, making me wonder if there was anything she wasn't automatically good at. The resulting quiet revealed a faint scraping of claw against stone up ahead in the distance. I also saw a hint of light. Even with my dimmed sight, movement snagged on my attention like hooks in canvas. Or one of those infernal laser pointers.

Speed was the only way we'd catch our quarry. I went on, lengthening my stride and facing my ears full forward. Olivia followed, her shorter legs meaning she had to let go of my hand. That was fine with me. If the wolf pounced, it'd get me, and she'd have a chance to shoot. But I wondered what good copper arrows would do against something allergic to silver.

Fortunately, we were in a tunnel, not a barrow or network of caves. The floor was even, definitely paved with something better than cobblestone. My strides ate the distance to that glimmer ahead. I heard a faint scrabble again, then the earthy thuds of a heavy animal cantering on bare earth.

I broke into a flat-out run, racing from the tunnel like a whiskered idiot, and got clocked in the head by something cold and slobbery with gamy-scented fur.

"Gah!" I had to fall, so I did it with a purpose. Tuck and roll, defend the neck and belly, then try to stand. Going prone in any battle was a death sentence, and I couldn't afford those anymore.

I stood facing a wolf over half my height, the light patches on its brindled fur reflecting the moonlight. A long, low growl twinged my whiskers. My tail flicked. I felt like an Unseelie gunslinger at Low Noon, except I wasn't armed. Not for a fight like this, anyway. I belonged to a shifter pack with a wolf Alpha and hadn't carried silver since joining it.

But I had my reliable old wits. I remembered the king's gifts. I reached toward the button, wondering if there was anything in the history of either world more absurd than a kitty cat facing down a werewolf with a silver button, and then the button morphed in my hand.

I held a dagger that was weighted perfectly for my grip and preferred fighting stance. I blinked. If this wolf was a Fed, I didn't want to kill him. There'd be consequences outside the Under, and anyway, the guy hadn't done anything to me. He'd come to Rhode Island in response to my anonymous tip, after all. But the dagger might make him keep his distance.

"Hold it!" Olivia stepped between us, pointing the business end of her bow at the mystery wolf. The tip of her arrow gleamed in the moonlight, silver as the night was long.

"But that's supposed to be my bane." The words were for Olivia, even though my eyes never left the wolf's. "How's it silver now?"

"It's part of what I am."

"Huh?"

"The king told me I can change the arrows into whatever's best to fight a given enemy as long as I fire them in the Under. There's no time to tell you more."

I shut my mouth before it caught the faerie equivalent of flies. My godmother hadn't lied, technically. She'd mentioned cat shifters, copper being my bane, and the Garters, and I'd snagged the first assumption in my claws like an awkward kitten. Kiki's half-truths two, Tony Gitano zero.

"Leave the king's demesne, and I won't have to use this." Olivia glared down the shaft of her arrow. "I'm giving you ten seconds."

The wolf whined, looking up at me. I shrugged, flicking my

tail deliberately this time. I couldn't help it; the shifter should have turned tail faced with two silver-armed opponents. He wasn't trapped. The way east was clear. And then, I understood half of everything.

"He needs our help." I lowered the dagger but kept it and my stance at the ready. "You can't run to the queen, can you?"

The wolf whined again. He thumped his tail twice, eyes going all melty like a puppy's, except gold with blue flecks. Where had I seen a werewolf with eyes like that before?

"But he can't stay here." Olivia shook her head. "If we fail the Quest, the king basically owns us."

"Yeah, okay. I get that." My whiskers twinged, the idea my thoughts chased more exciting than a low-noon pizza. "What did the king say your Quest was, exactly?"

"He said—" Olivia's eyes widened. "Oh. Tony, you're a genius!"

"No way the Goblin King would say a thing like that," I mumbled. I cleared my throat and put on my best outside voice. "What did the king say?"

"He said, and I quote, 'There's a creature there without my permission. That cannot be.'" Olivia eased back on the bowstring and smiled.

Something thudded against the ground, kicking ruddy fallen leaves into the air. I chuckled. The werewolf's tail, of course. He was definitely pondering what we were pondering.

"So we get his permission, *capisce*?" The sides of my face ached, kind of like how your arms or legs might after a good workout. I barely ever smiled, but this adventure changed all that.

"You should smile more often, you know." Olivia nudged me with an elbow. "It looks good on you."

"Keep on saying things like that, and I'll never stop."

"Oh, but you will. You'll stop everything soon."

I didn't need to turn around, didn't need my new ability to sense magic, either. I knew by the powdered oil scent of a gun under fine wool and that infuriatingly warm tenor who was behind us.

"Coming to work with your kid is the first and worst sign of helicopter parenting." I turned around to see my father surrounded by the fuzzy frame of a portal from the mundane world to the Under. I wondered how he'd managed that until I saw him holding a magipsychic device he'd taken as payment in a Black Market deal. "Or haven't you heard?"

"No, but I have heard about your bird."

"You did not just go there." Olivia's voice almost covered the sound of her turning around. I glanced over my shoulder to see that she'd aimed her bow again. This time, the arrow wasn't tipped with silver or even copper as I'd expected. It smelled like wood and glowed green.

"Don't make me laugh." Dad laughed anyway, his hand going to his shoulder holster and coming back with a silenced pistol. "That old toy won't kill me. I will, however, kill *you*."

"I know." Olivia aimed directly at his chest and let fly, leaving herself undefended.

"I love you." The words I'd held back from Olivia Adler all this time were finally free. I refused to be too late for her to hear them this time. Never mind that I'd never hear them back because I was about to bite it for the ninth time.

I jumped up between Olivia and my father, the copper-tipped bullet landing smack between two of the ribs on the right side of my chest. I felt the pain like a million wasp stings as it blew through skin and bone and went out the other side. Blood flew from my mouth as I tried to breathe, but my lung was shot through on two sides. I couldn't get air, and could barely even get a scent. But I could still see.

The not-copper arrow buried itself in my father's right shoulder. He laughed and pulled it out, and the wound closed. The hole in his suit's dark fabric showed his skin up like an eclipse through a pinhole projector.

I dropped to my knees, then fell face-first on the ground. There'd been no question about putting myself between the woman I'd given my eighth and ninth life for and the murderous thug who'd sired me. My sight left me, but I heard one more thing.

"I love you too, Tony." Olivia's hand on my shoulder felt like ice, then fire, then comfort, then nothing.

I was adrift, not freezing like when Kiki had woken me. I hadn't expected any pearly gates, but there was a name for the closest concept the religious set has to where I was.

"Limbo." My voice didn't sound like anything. I wasn't sure there was such a thing as sound in that place. I tested it again. "This blows."

"It does nothing, actually."

The voice came from nowhere and everywhere at the same time. I wondered whether that was how I sounded, but what got my curiosity even more tightly gripped was another question.

"Who?"

"There's no easy answer to that question." The voice had a little lilt to it but nothing whatsoever that hinted at age, gender, or creature type. I just had to settle.

"Okay. Why?"

"You've made a big sacrifice for someone of extreme importance."

"Thanks and all, but," I waved what I thought might be my hand, "underwhelming doesn't begin to describe this."

The voice chuckled. "So, then. What is It you seek after your ninth life and death?"

"It with a capital I?"

"Aye."

"Well, if it's all the same, I'd rather go back to Olivia than anywhere else they say people go when they die."

"One condition."

"Anything."

"In the very near future, you'll have the chance to stop someone from gaining power. Don't."

I thought of my father and wasn't sure I could live up to my end of that bargain. I'd been stealing from him for years because I didn't believe in arms races, but the memory of Olivia's voice, the last words I'd heard her say, made me believe that maybe great power could be used responsibly. I felt like there were two of me. Old Tony wasn't up to that challenge, but New Tony was a whole different cat. New Tony might also be extremely limited because he'd probably be a ghost. Something about that didn't feel right, though. At any rate, I was ready to answer.

"I can do it."

"Then return whence you came, renewed."

The pungent odor of crushed grass and old leaves met my nose. I took an honest to goodness breath. Staring at the ground was no good, so I pushed off and sat up. When I blinked, the number nine appeared on the inside of my eyelids. I did it again, and the numeral persisted.

"So that's what they meant by renewed. Wow."

"Tony!" Arms and feathers surrounded me, Olivia's cheek pressed against mine. This was Heaven, and if I wasn't mistaken, I had nine more lives left to experience it with.

"Damn kid." My father still stood on the other side of the portal, pointing his gun at the ground.

"Will you shoot again, Dad?"

"Nah. The silencer's busted." My father wore an expression I'd never seen before. It reminded me of the time I'd snuck in to see *The Sixth Sense* in the theater. At the end of the movie, all the people had the same dazed and bemused look now appearing on my father's face.

"What was that arrow, Olivia?" I turned to look at her.

"Arrow of truth." She grinned. "It works for Wonder Woman's lasso. Why not the Gamayun and her magic bow?"

"Huh." I blinked.

"Miss Adler's a rare bird." Dad's voice made my tail stand up, all the hairs on end. I hadn't expected an answer from him. "The neutral magical bird shifter."

"They're extinct, though." I shook my head. "Legends."

"So are Kells Cats." Dad's eyes narrowed in a greedy glare I knew too well. "And one of those has been dangled in front of me like a fish on a line for over twenty years. That was why I got so pissed when your body vanished. I must have miscounted the times you died. That house falling on you should have been nine, so shooting you was extra credit. I don't know why you're still sucking wind. I want the ear that gives you your power."

"But why?" I couldn't understand. A Kells Cat's ear wouldn't do him any good. Those neutral magic shifter pieces only worked on people born in the Under.

"Ask him where Cassandra Spanos has been all this time." Olivia's glare was sharp and palpable. "Ask why she's put on weight, while you're at it."

"Oh, no, Dad." I shook my head. "You didn't."

"I made sure my second son was born in the queen's castle." Dad smiled. "Not a hole in the ground like you two."

"I'll have you know that the Royal Howe is no mere hole in the ground. It's special in ways that bend the rules between courts nearly to their breaking points." The Goblin King strode forward, hand on the hilt of his sword. "But a pretender to Roman greatness can wait for my attention. My champion will direct me as to the fate of the interloper."

"Your Highness," Olivia made the most graceful curtsy ever done while holding a nocked bow. "This interloper wishes to ask your permission to remain in your demesne."

"Does he now?" The king's eyebrow tilted upward. "He shall have to speak for himself."

The wolf shifter sat up and begged. His whine carried more than just canine noises, even though I couldn't have deciphered it in a million years. The king chuckled. Of course, he spoke wolfanese.

"Champion, you are released from my service. For now." The king put his hands together in a series of slow claps, as though we'd finished nineteen holes on the fairway instead of a Quest in the Under. "Derek Dennison, you have my permission to remain here until you choose to leave. If you should return, however, I expect to hear of it with haste."

"He can use my portal here if he wants." Dad's brief grin went as sour as moldy cheese. "I'll kill him the second he gets to this side, though."

"I commend you for your newfound honesty, Gino." The king inclined his head. "I am sure my former wife and her suitor will appreciate it immensely, especially once they understand your true opinion of them."

"No." Dad reminded me of the first guy I saw insulting him. That fellow turned up dead in the bay three months later.

"What's wrong, Dad?" I asked. "You can take those two, right?"

"I can't." He looked like an empty balloon. "But you. You and your punk kid friends. You could hide me, son."

"But I won't." I shook my head. "I'm on the right side of the law, remember? Hiding fugitives isn't the kind of thing I should be doing."

"I bet Extrahuman Witness Protection would help, though." Olivia's voice carried a flood of sincere concern. I wasn't surprised. She'd see the good in a discarded candy wrapper if it needed help. As unrealistic as that was in my dad's case, I loved her for it. "If you offer to help put Hopewell away, they'll protect you."

"I'm no rat." Dad's left hand reached for his pocket. "Good luck finding me."

The magic holding his portal open started fading. I didn't even have to look at Olivia for agreement. The time for questioning her trust was over. We jumped, and Derek bounded after.

CHAPTER FOURTEEN

Olivia

I stumbled when we landed, nearly toppling onto Derek Dennison in his wolf form. Tony didn't. Cats really do always land on their feet. I wondered how he'd managed that with his tail, ears, and whiskers vanishing once we stepped into the mortal realm. He must have been prepared for that eventuality. I had been, too. In error.

An updraft coming off the water righted me. I still had my partially shifted extras. It finally occurred to me that although Tony had cat features besides his tail, I only had wings in the Under. I shook off the unintended woolgathering. Gino Gitano was getting away. I pulled my phone from the pockets that had replaced my satchel when the king upgraded our clothes and started a message to all the right people.

"Dad, wait!" Tony took a step forward.

"Not when you got that pigsticker, I won't." Gino stepped back as fast as a suburban power-walker with his hands up in front of him.

"Um." Tony looked down at the copper dagger in his hand,

then stuck it in the post to my left. "Changed my mind. I'll help hide you if you cooperate with the police."

"You make no sense at all, you know that?" Gino shook his head. "What do you want to help me for?"

"Because you're my dad." Tony paced toward his father, hands out to his sides. "Because even though you've been a right criminal bastard, we're still blood. My godmother said Mom loved you. There has to be some good in you still if that's true."

"You met the crazy fox bitch, then. Good." Gino chuckled and stopped, then put his hands down. "She's not what she says she is, you know. And yeah, your mother loved me. I loved her. But you came along and ruined all that."

"What?" Tony froze.

"Celestina was my moon and stars. Mine." His voice lowered to a threatening rumble, like a distant thunderstorm. "The second she went into labor, she stole that Kells ear from me and ran to the Under, tithed to that fool of a king. Your mother, a Sidhe changeling, went Unseelie because she saw in some vision that she had to. For your sake."

"She was a Precog?" Tony's shoulders drooped. I wanted to do something, say something to comfort him, but he needed to hear this, and I would not interrupt. I finished my text message instead. "You never told me that. Or anything else about her, either."

"You didn't deserve to know anything about her! You ruined her and ruined us!" Gino's hands made fists like small boulders.

"How?"

"By existing." Tony's father took a step toward him. "She loved you more. She was yours before you even took your first breath. You stole my Celestina's heart from me, and I'll hate you forever for it."

Tony staggered back as though his father's words were physical blows. I understood exactly the kind of man Gino Gitano was now, even though I'd hoped for better. Did Tony? I tapped Send.

Tony

"Did you ever think there might be some other reason?" I tried to stand up straight, throw my shoulders back, and knock off all the chips on them in the process. Instead, I barely managed to keep my voice from cracking. "Maybe Mom stopped loving you because you're a jealous, possessive meathead with homicidal tendencies."

"Those things never bothered her before." Dad showed his teeth. "Tina was a survivor. She understood the Reveal was changing everything. It was why she chose the strongest mate." He looked past me at Olivia and smirked. "You take after her in that, at least." He chuckled. "Gamayun. That's power big enough to make your Kells Cat shtick look like a lame duck in comparison, but nothing you do will ever make up for how you turned your mother on me. You made it so she had to die and leave me stuck with you. You're not the son I wanted."

"I never was. Never will be." I managed to drag my gaze up from that creepy grin to his eyes. He'd said things like that before, implying it was my fault he'd killed Mom. "And here's a big surprise. I care about that. I care way too much about your thoughts and feelings."

Dad chuckled, the sound tapering into the rumbling purr he always let loose when he knew he'd won. But he didn't know jack. He held his right hand cocked, inches from the copper-loaded gun at his hip.

"It ain't healthy. You make noises like everything's my fault, and you even believe it, but none of that's true. Now it's time to put the blame where it belongs. I grew up twisted, scared of my own shadow. Hinky, they called me. Because of you." I hung on his gaze and used it, clawed my way up from the half-crouch he'd cornered me into for most of my life. I watched his eyes widen, almost missing the tremor in his right hand. "And that. Ends. Now."

I stood straight and tall, his scowl roiling around me like fog in the darkest hour of the night. I let him sulk and grumble, the fact that all his words were true unable to cut me down. Because of him, I knew darkness. But because of Olivia, I knew it died with the light, and there was none harsher than truth and justice. None brighter than love and friendship.

High-beams cut across the grass, the wet crunch and smack of tires on damp pavement a counterpoint to Derek's growl. Dad's smoke-and-shadows act burned away as he turned away from me.

"Mister Gitano, you're a material witness in an open investigation." A pair of slender shadows bisected the headlights, one about my height and the other nearly six feet tall. "I also suspect you've got key information on a case currently at trial. I've got a subpoena."

"Good luck keeping me alive to honor that." Dad's left shoulder hitched in a shrug.

"I just happen to have Luck in abundance." The shorter figure moved closer, and I made out his face. Yoshi Ichiro. Olivia had called her employer to deal with the Mafia boss. "Come with me if you want protection."

"Said it before, I'm no rat."

"This isn't about any alleged connection to illegal imports and exports, sir." I recognized the voice. Albert Dunstable. "This is about catching a bigger fish."

"I know that fish. He's one cold shark. You either join him or sleep with other specimens of the scaly and water breathing variety if you know what I'm saying."

"All the same, we can protect you if you agree to help us."

"Wait." The word barked out sharp, like a blade on a chalkboard.

Derek Dennison stood there on two legs, one hand holding a branch that blocked everything from his waist to his thighs from view. Thank goodness. I remembered him now.

"You're Josh's missing older brother." I looked from him to my father. I already knew the answer to my question, but Dad didn't. "Why should the best extrahuman defense attorney wait for a scrub werewolf without a stitch to his name?"

"Because this scrub belongs to the FBE, kid." Derek coughed. "Ichiro and Dunstable made a nice offer, but they need law enforcement supervision when dealing with someone like your Dad here, and I'm one of the agents assigned to this whole mess."

"Good points." I smirked. "Sorry for calling you a scrub."

"Nah, it's good." Derek waved his free hand. "Anyway, we'd better be going."

He strode toward the car, somehow managing to snag Dad by the arm and making it look easy. All the hair went up on the back of my neck. Everything would have been different if Derek hadn't got stuck in the Under instead of being free to investigate since the spring. Maybe Wilfred Harcourt would still be alive. Maybe Josh and company would have had more help with everything that came after, too.

"Just call your parents," I called after him. "Your brother and sister, too."

"Well, duh." Derek had his back to me, but I still thought I could hear his eyes roll.

Ichiro got in the driver's seat while Derek ushered my father into the back. Albert Dunstable had his hand on the front passenger door, about to pull the handle.

"Wait, Al!" Olivia ran forward. "Can you stick around for a minute?"

"I suppose." He stepped away from the car, waving at its occupants. After it pulled out and drove off, he met us halfway between the monument and the parking lot. "What's this about, then?"

"I have something for you." Olivia rummaged in one pocket of her feathered skirt. "If only I could remember where I put it."

"Hold on," Al chewed his lower lip, his eyebrows drawing a line in his forehead between them. "Is that Unseelie adventuring gear you're wearing?"

"Watch it, Al." I made a cutting motion with my fingers. "Ix-nay on the estions-quay."

"Hmm." One of Al's eyebrows avoided the imminent confrontation with its opposite by lifting halfway between his eye and his hairline. "You have magic now. So, you're tithed to the king."

"Um, no." Olivia blinked, her hand finally out of her pocket and curled around a garishly colored piece of paper. "This magic isn't faerie. It's older. I only put high-ranking faeries into debt with questions. You're just a knight, Al. You're good. The king told me that as the Gamayun, I'm a free agent, like Kells Cats and Kitsunes."

"So you're not the Sirin. Good. One of us would have to leave the law firm if that were the case. Too much risk of monarchal wrath."

"What to the who now?" Being left out of the loop bugged me even more than the confusion that came with it.

"You study faerie history, and you've never heard of the three magic birds?" Al blinked. "I find that hard to believe."

"Of course, I've heard of them." I shook my head. "But only the Alkonost has been active recently. The Sirin feather is around somewhere." I wasn't about to tell them about the thing in my pocket. "The Gamayun feather vanished."

"Like Kitsunes vanished, right?" Olivia sighed. "Hoo, boy. They're trinket bearers like you and me. You get an ear. Kitsunes get tails. We get feathers. But I didn't call Al back for a history lecture. Your dad wasn't bluffing."

Another car approached, turning its lights off at a respectable distance this time. I tried not to peer into the darkness after it. Familiar voices got louder and closer. I smelled vampire, bear, and human, and felt the tingle of Psychic energy in the air and a prickle of magic. The magic felt light, but worn as though with use. Whoever the Magus was, it had to be a professor, not a student. I wondered which faculty member my pack would drag to a cemetery in the middle of the night, then shut my curiosity inside a box.

I didn't bother waiting for Tinfoil Hat's arrival. Instead, I turned to watch Olivia hand Al the paper. I recognized it. The kid's drawing of herself and her mom and grandpa that Kiki had been trying to steal. As the Sidhe's hand met the flimsy newsprint, his hair blew back even though there wasn't any wind. What little color he had left his face.

"You'll tell me where you got this, Olivia."

"I can only tell you that deep down, you already know who it came from."

"So say it."

"It's not my place to say." Olivia smiled gently. "I'm just a messenger."

"Why bother bringing something you can't explain?"

She probably would have answered, but after that, everything went sideways.

CHAPTER FIFTEEN

Olivia

"Move!" I leaped into the air, using my wings to maneuver between the newly opened portal and Tony and Al. I had some crazy idea that I could shield them both with my wings the way Blaine had described shielding Jeannie and Kimiko from bullets six months earlier. But I was a bird, not an armor-plated dragon. I'd get shot to bits.

At that moment, I didn't care. Nothing in the universe could make me go through losing Tony again.

No projectiles tore through my feathers. No bullets riddled my back.

"Turn around." Tony glared at something over my shoulder, someone who invoked as much negative emotion in him as his father.

"Fine." I did as he asked, keeping my wings outstretched just to be on the safe side.

"I always hated that insipid rhyme about the owl and the pussy-cat." Richard Hopewell's sneer looked as sharp as the knife he held to Kiki's throat. "And I am sick and tired of you meddling kids escaping death all the time. It's even worse when I consider how much I hate your elders with their 'magic for everyone' agenda."

"Karen, no!" Henrietta Thurston looked older than usual, the gray in her hair more pronounced, and her posture stooped and cowering. The anguish in her voice startled me almost as much as the unfamiliar name she'd given to Tony's godmother.

"Hi, Hen. Ow!" Kiki's attempt at a parade wave got cut off by Richard Hopewell's knife pressing closer to her neck.

"Listen here, you sorry excuse for a Scooby-Doo villain," Tony's voice drawled, the letter R dropping like hot potatoes. "You let go of my godmother, or there'll be hell to pay."

"Karen Thurston and I go way back." Richard chuckled. "She was one of my earliest experiments in mind magic manipulation. In fact, she used to babysit Henry and me back in the day, although I doubt either of them remember much about that. Right, Henry?"

Henry Baxter clenched his fists and hissed, his fangs gleaming in the moonlight. I didn't want to think about the threats Richard had made to coerce Henry into wiping or replacing Kiki's memories.

"Your father is a much more suitable partner, Antonio." Richard grinned, then pointed one finger on the hand gripping Kiki at Henry. "Henry has talent but not the stomach for most of my interests." He chuckled. "Had, I should say."

We scattered as a gout of flame erupted from the tip of his finger in Henry's general direction. The odor of singed leather and hair mingled with crushed grass and exclamations of alarm. I helped Henry up. He held something oval and smooth and cooler to the touch than his hand. A memory charm.

"Remember," he said.

Images crashed against the pillars of my memory like waves against Newport's famous craggy cliffs, things years of therapy hadn't revealed. Henry's memory charm raised the curtain on that lost swath of childhood from before I got adopted.

A woman with stark white hair and even brighter rainbow wings smiled down at me, holding my hand as I hopped around a bare hill beside her. The memory was worn and faded, like old reel-to-reel film, so I couldn't make out the words in her coos of encouragement. The love and pride were all there, increasing each time my wings caught air during one of my jumps. Now I knew why learning to ride a bike had inspired frequent bouts of déjà vu.

In the memory, I giggled, glancing off toward the tree line. Two sets of eyes watched from the shadows. One stayed put, her red hair and garb doing little to camouflage her even in the autumnal foliage. The other advanced, bringing a boy about my age into clear view. His hair was black, and unruly waves tossed around a pair of ears the same color. He stalked me, crouched. I pretended not to notice him until the moment before he pounced. We fell together, laughing and kicking up fallen leaves until a doorway appeared in the side of the hill and our mothers called us in. The boy's was tall and pale with hair the color of coal. The fox woman followed us, head turning to look back as she went. I recognized her as Kiki although she only had two tails.

The memory changed, accompanied by a feeling of falling backward. The world in my eyes shone in whorls and loops of color without context, blurred lines, and vague shapes. The voices rang clear and pure, all three familiar.

"They won't have an easy time. No one will trust him until the last possible moment, and she won't begin trusting herself until she returns to the Under." That was the other baby's mom.

"But are they safe enough?" My heart felt full to bursting with love at the sound of my own mother's voice.

"Not yet." The other baby's mom sighed. "They'll need time

here, more than double the amount I can stay, even with this Howe bending the rules to let us live here together."

"I'll protect him, then." The fox woman's voice made me squeak with mirth. "Least I can do after all my failures."

"Henny won't stay mad at you forever, Karen," my mother said.

"Notice that the Precog didn't offer any reassurances," said the fox woman.

"Fine, have some." The other mom chuckled, but when she spoke again, her voice sounded sad. "She'll remember this at the right time and help save your life someday."

The colors went dark and the voices faded until only the sound of crackling flames remained in my ears. Singed fabric and burnt leather offended my nostrils. I turned my head to check on everyone else.

Lynn huddled behind Bobby, while Bianca and Lane stood behind some kind of magical shield blossoming out of Henrietta Thurston's wand. Her magic pushed back the flames still pouring from Richard Hopewell's finger.

"Enough!" Albert Dunstable's voice tolled like a grim bell as he strode forward to confront the Extramagus. "Her Majesty will think little of you setting fire to Swan Point Cemetery."

"She'll have no trouble with me battling an old flame." Richard chuckled, but I noticed that the flames died down.

"That may well be, but it's wise to be more careful." Al put his hands on his hips. "Some of these are friends of her court."

"Friends of knights and pages, you mean." Richard scoffed. "Little consequence. And that one there is my enemy, just like these." He pointed his wand at Bianca, then me, then Tony.

"This isn't the Under." Al shook his head. "You can't go bringing the queen's justice here."

"You are not one to say where her justice belongs."

"I'm my mother's son and heir." Al tilted his chin up, looking down his nose at Richard Hopewell. "She's consequential. And the queen has charged her with navigating the legal differences between this realm and hers. If I say you are overstepping, you are."

Except I knew Al was bluffing. Mortal law hadn't stopped the queen from seeking her own justice before; recently too. Richard backed off anyway.

"I'm claiming my right as Her Majesty's suitor to bring one of these back with me to justice."

"Your right to such a thing is shaky, Mr. Hopewell." Al crossed his arms over his chest. "You still haven't tithed."

"I'm still not worthy enough." Richard's smile shone like bleached bone. "Maybe bringing one of these troublemakers back will let me prove myself."

Al's mouth opened, then closed. "Maybe the queen has other priorities," he attempted.

Richard only laughed. He changed his grip on Kiki, bringing his wand arm around her, so he had the business end pointing at her face. Then, he brought the knife down and around into the space between him and her.

Kiki's voice ripped the darkness above our heads apart. Tears doused her face like a sudden rainstorm. I smelled blood.

Lane Meyer turned, staring in horror at Henry Baxter. I could tell right away that the Psychic vampire needed blood badly after his injuries. His fangs were out, and his eyes glinted with a baleful light. He paced toward the wounded Kitsune like a hungry lion.

"Henry, no!" Lane tried rushing to stop his friend, but Henrietta's barrier hadn't dissipated.

"Karen!" Henrietta just stood there, and all the color in her face drained as she watched, unable to act. "Get your hands off my aunt, Dick!"

"You won't be able to call anyone names for much longer, Etta." Richard's words were punctuated by wet tearing sounds.

"I got a name for you. Pincushion." Tony stood behind

Richard with a silver dagger in one hand and the copper one in the other. The Extramagus hadn't managed to activate his personal wards. I glanced aside to see that Tony must have retrieved his other dagger while I wasn't looking. "Let my godmother go."

"Fine." Richard pushed Kiki with one hand and dropped his knife with the other. She stumbled several paces, sprawling on the ground near the Headmistress' feet. "I got what I came for." He held a bundle of tails in his knife hand, the weapon at his feet slick with blood. "And I let go of her, too. Now I'll finish the job." He pointed the wand at the prone Kitsune.

"No." Henrietta Thurston stepped between her aunt and her nemesis. She waved her wand, erecting the shield over Kiki and removing it from Lane and Bianca in the process. Henry beat against it with both fists until Lane pulled him away. "Mr. Meyer, open a portal. Banish him to the queen's demesne. Now."

"Okay." Lane frowned at a spot just above Richard's right shoulder, then belted out a single wailing note. A half-light that reminded me of the ocean horizon where we'd met Gemma grew behind the evil Extramagus. Tony bounded toward the monument so he wouldn't get caught in the portal. Richard only laughed and brandished the bundle of bloody Kitsune tails. I watched his wards shimmer into existence around him.

"Don't let him take those!" Gemma Tolland's voice rang out at a volume that would have carried through a nor'easter. She surged forth on the back of a black Kelpie, her daughter clinging on in front of her. The pirate captain's charge from behind the Fishman Memorial's bulk called me to action.

I ran forward, raising my wings as I rushed Richard Hopewell. I staggered back a moment later when his wand exuded a blast of icy air that slammed past me and into Headmistress Thurston's car, flipping it over. He'd made a big mistake, though. I used the remnants of his attack against him, rising into the air on the back of his magic.

Shooting up to a respectable height while drawing my bow was the hard part. Aiming and dive-bombing the Extramagus was easy, but outside the Under, my arrows were mundane. I screeched, the force behind the sound laced with magic, as it had been when I broke the dorm window escaping from Gino. Wards shimmered around Richard, both the magic and the Psychic wavering at my cry. Would my attack be enough to stop him?

Tony

I watched Olivia fall, her downward arc bringing back the first time I'd seen her in the Under on her mission of mercy to rescue Gee-Nome. I nearly mistook her for an angel again this time, too. An avenging one.

She wouldn't be able to hurt Richard. His wards had wavered under her screech, but they hadn't collapsed completely. He looked up, though, distracted.

The bones in my lower back rearranged themselves, skin itching as my tail furred over. I welcomed the return of my ears, whiskers, and tail, waiting a moment for the rest of my body to follow. It didn't. All the agility and heightened senses of my cat form, none of the wimpy size and strength drawbacks. Bonus: I got to keep my hands and the weapons in them. I didn't grow wings, though. Those must be for use in the Under only.

I let the copper dagger drop from my right hand. Falling on my own bane ain't a mistake to make twice.

My feet barely touched the dewy grass, making almost no sound as I dashed forward, arms behind me for extra speed. I leaped, left foot landing on one point of the anchor sculpture as I used it to get some air and avoid Olivia's arrow.

I managed the feat and reached out with both hands. The dagger in my left glanced harmlessly off Richard's wrist just like I knew it would, but I got the result I wanted. He dropped my godmother's tails.

Snatching the magical artifacts with my right hand before they hit the ground was tricky, but I managed. I stumbled, though. One sneaker snagging the stub of a discarded vigil candle. Done in by my own fake memorial.

Before I ate dirt, something caught me by the back of my trench coat. Some*one*. Olivia. She coasted up and then back down again, setting us at Henrietta's side. I held the bundle of tails out to her. She blinked but took them, turning them over in her hands a few times. The stench of ozone filled my nostrils, yet no light or sound struck in my immediate area.

I watched Richard stagger forward two steps, then back one. Blinding sunlight shone on the other side of Lane's portal. My Nocturnal Studies major didn't give me much information about the queen's side of things, but I knew she kept her residence eternally at high noon. Lane's knowledge of portals came from Margot, who was a Seelie Summoner. Of course, anything he opened here would go to the queen's demesne. Her pet Extramagus would end up practically in her lap.

Except he wasn't going to. Evil was as tenacious as black mold, and Richard's brand was no exception. Someone would have to take a risk, push him in. Whoever did that could end up dragged in with him and have to endure his rage on the other side.

I stepped forward when an arm, pale and thin but cold like a lead pipe, stopped me.

"Allow us." Bianca's grin wasn't entirely her own. I could tell that she and her ghost friend Horace were doing their Possession thing.

"You'll fall in." I opened my mouth again, about to say something stupid like I'd do it myself. But that was last week's Tony, the one with a life or two left to spare. The one who felt unworthy of help, of friendship. That side of me wasn't gone, but it never would be if I didn't resist and do something new. I shut my yap and let the living dead girl talk.

"Nah." The Possessed medium gave me a combined smile. "We're strong as a lion together."

"Then we all go." Olivia peered at me from Bianca and Horace's other side. Having her on my side all but guaranteed eventual victory over my old habits. "Lion plus two."

We nodded at each other and rushed forward. Olivia's wings gave extra leverage while the Bianca/Horace duo pushed with force that matched my dad on one of his good days. Richard gave ground. I held my action. Good thing, too. He aimed his wand at Olivia.

"Boot to the hand!" I matched actions to words. Except for the boot part. I'll always be a sneakers kind of guy.

The length of wood tumbled through the air, end over end. Something followed it, a shimmering feather so bright I couldn't make out the color. Richard chuckled. I turned.

He had the ghost-Possessed medium by the wrists. Olivia had them by a satchel strap and the back of Bianca's paisley peasant top. Olivia flapped her wings, trying to get airborne. It didn't happen. Richard didn't have to work too hard. He'd given up trying to escape the portal, and its leverage outstripped Olivia's.

Fabric tore. They fell through. The portal closed, but someone stood where it had been. I remembered.

"Horace died here. He can't go to the Under without a monarch's permission."

"She'll make it." Al reached out a hand. He didn't pat Olivia's back or shoulder. I guessed he didn't want to get whacked in the face with a wing.

"She won't." Olivia's voice came out all strangled. I saw what she held in her lap.

"That's her insulin in there." I whirled, about to lay into Lane Meyer and demand that he open another portal and get her back, even though I knew he was all out of Psychic mojo. I would have, too, a week earlier. But not after I saw his face.

Lane's expression was flatter than a week-old soda. His knees wobbled and he held on to Henry like the blood-deprived vamp was a lifeline and not a threat to anything with a pulse. He looked like Blaine had on the day of his stepdad's funeral.

Old Tony would have chewed him out, but I had to be New Tony. Being a better friend wasn't just for when the chips were up.

"It ain't your fault, Lane. The Extramagus is a literal and figurative Dick." I glanced at Horace's ghost, who was staring at the spot where the portal had been. I had some idea of how Olivia must have felt when I died that ninth time. "And anyway, Ed's on the Seelie side of the Under right now. Maybe he can make sure Bianca's okay. Can you get him on the secret decoder ring or whatever you use to communicate?"

"I'll take care of it." Al Dunstable turned his back and walked a short distance away.

Lynn and Bobby came rushing back from the flipped car, carrying a cooler between them. They set it down next to Lane and Henry. Both of them needed a drink or three by then, but I had something else to do.

"Kiki, you okay?" I wrinkled my nose. "Why do I still smell blood?"

"Because that monster cut off my actual tail. I let you assume, but I'm not a Kitsune." My godmother held a wad of blood-soaked fabric against her backside. I barely recognized the sash she'd recently worn around her waist to hide all the tails. "Just your average fox shifter. I collected the tails and they gave me magic because I come from a family with Kitsune blood, but I wasn't born in the Under. I can't bind them to myself in anything but a literal sense."

"Hoo, boy." Olivia tilted her head, peering at my godmother. Her hand brushed against mine. "So, Kitsunes really are extinct."

The sadness in Olivia's voice moved me to put my arm around her shoulders. Even with the wings, it wasn't awkward. Her arm went around my waist, and her cheek pressed to my chest just below my collarbone.

"They're not." Henrietta Thurston stood up, reaching behind her head to unbind her hair. "I'm Karen's blood kin, and like the two of you, I was born in the Under."

The hair tumbling down the Headmistress's back and around her shoulders had no more gray in it. The light brown took on ruddy tones. She smiled as seven tails waved out from behind her.

"Your ex is so screwed." I slapped a hand over my mouth. "Sorry."

"Don't be. He is." Henrietta's smile managed to get toothier and scarier. "The next time he shows his face anywhere near my school or the kids in it, he's getting a blast of Foxfire he won't soon forget."

"Mama!" We all turned at the sound of the child's voice.

Hope Tolland stood at the spot where Richard's wand had landed. She wasn't pointing at the magical instrument. Instead, she had her finger nearly on the bright object he'd thrown. A feather. I felt the object in my pocket, the piece of obsidian carved so it could have been the dark fraternal twin of that other feather. Its energy was decidedly Unseelie. The thing on the ground was its opposite.

"No, kid!" I let go of Olivia and ran toward Gemma's daughter but then I stopped, remembering the promise I'd made that brought me back to life. The kid was about to gain power and I couldn't keep her from it, no matter how badly being separated from her mother would hurt her in the long run. I made myself a promise to look out for the kid. At least she'd have someone around who knew that kind of pain.

Hope's finger met the bright feather, her mouth open as if to scream. A sound came out, saccharine for the ears, a song unheard in the mortal world for over two decades, by my calculations. Her eyes widened. I was close enough to hear the creak of reforming bone, but no one missed her emerging wings. They glowed with a rainbow of colors, feathers shimmering even in the scant light of a cemetery at night.

"Hope!" Gemma dashed toward her daughter. I held her back, not an easy feat with a statuesque troll.

"You can't, Gemma." I shook my head, hissing as I dug my heels in. "Because you feel it, right? You're Unseelie, and she's the opposite of that now. You'll both get put to death."

"But she's my baby," Gemma said. She choked down a sob and leaned away from me. "Who's going to take care of her?"

"Mama?" Hope held her hands up, her wings stretching to their full span on either side of her. The kid's hair caught the light from her wings.

Olivia stepped forward, giving me another bout of déjà vu. I glanced at Kiki, who was smiling up at her.

"No, baby." Gemma swallowed another sob. "You can't come with me this time. Or ever." The grief finally put a stopper in her voice. She looked at me, but her eyes cut to Al for a moment. "You'll have to go and meet the queen."

I knew, of course. Like most of my intel, I'd found out by being in the right place while hiding from my father. I couldn't help. I'd promised not to tell, with the weight of the Under backing that promise, but now the cat was about to get out of the bag.

I wiped my face, and my fingers came away wet. Something sharp and heavy at the same time grew in my chest, painful, like the copper dagger the last time I died. A memory crashed the gate in my mind. This had happened to me next to a Gnomehill, not in this graveyard with symbols of hope all around. My mother had walked away from me, just like Gemma was going to have to do now. But she'd had people to leave me with, women she knew and trusted. And a friend about my age.

A slender arm slipped its way around my waist. Olivia. The piercing pressure lifted.

Al stepped up. This kid was gonna have it tough but not as bad as me. The Dunstables were just straight-laced, not monsters like Dad.

"I'll watch over her." The Sidhe bent at the waist, his white hair slipping over one shoulder as he peered into the kid's face. "Hmm. Hope. Not the name I would have chosen for my daughter but a fitting one all the same."

"Your what?" Olivia blinked. "Sidhe and troll changelings can't have owl shifter kids."

"My aunt was an owl shifter. She vanished in the Under not long after binding herself to a feather much like the one Hope has now." Al straightened, extending one hand toward the kid. "Hope can only be my child."

"Someone told you." Gemma went still, her limbs stiffening, and her gaze entirely on the Sidhe.

"No one did." Al sighed. "Nothing but plain old deduction. Everything about it makes sense, especially now that she ended up with the Alkonost's feather."

"Explain."

Al's eyes traveled slowly up and over Gemma, taking a good long view before settling on her face. I knew that game. I'd played it with Olivia for almost three years whenever I thought she couldn't see me. That was how you looked at someone you want and can't have. I'd had it bad. Albert Dunstable had it worse than me.

"How old are you, Hope?"

"I'll be six this winter, Sir."

"Six years, Gemma." Al shook his head, looking wearier than an ethereally handsome Sidhe ought to. "It's been more than six years since that graduation party. Since our promise."

"The promise you broke."

He stared past her at the figure next to the monument.

Gemma's grandfather looked almost as imposing as the sculpture. Al closed his eyes, his mouth a tight, straight line as though he fought any and all expression. "It couldn't be kept. I wasn't there then, but I'm here now. Let me know my daughter. Let me help."

"What other choice do I have?" Gemma dropped to one knee, fists clenched at her side. "Hope, I want you to go with your father."

"But Mama, I don't know him." The kid crossed her arms over her chest. "I wanna be with you."

"But you—"

"I know I can't, Mama." Her lower lip trembled, and a single tear slid down her cheek. "The magic's telling me so."

"Then go with Sir Albert." Gemma's face glistened in the faint light at the horizon. "Captain's orders."

"Yes, Mama."

"It's time to go, Gem." Admiral Tolland's voice projected clear and loud, probably a side-effect of decades at sea.

Gemma stood, turned her back on the lot of us, and paced toward her grandfather. They walked together toward the monument. A moment before they'd have bashed their heads on it, a portal opened. I recognized the dock by the king's lodge and saw Gemma look back, then it closed behind them. I knew she'd be back for her daughter at some point. Even the rift between courts couldn't break a love like the one between the troll and her child.

"I'm your prisoner now, Sir Knight." The kid's grave tone had me blinking back my own tears.

"You don't have to call me that." Al reached down, his hand inches above her head as though he wanted to ruffle her hair. He leaned over and took Bianca's satchel from Olivia instead. "And you're not my prisoner. I've promised your mother that I'd watch over and protect you. I'll have to do that at the queen's castle for now, however. Let me bring you there; get you settled, and introduced to your grandmother. Then I have some work to do here for a little while. I'll come back later in the day."

Hope only nodded, her gaze on the spot where her mother had disappeared.

I knew how she felt, but knew absolutely nothing about what I could do to help.

As it turned out, helping Hope and her family was someone else's story.

EPILOGUE

Ed

"I can't believe Kitsunes are making a comeback right here at PPC." Josh Dennison leaned forward, hunching over the back of his backward chair. "Neutral magical shifters with heirloom tokens seem to be all the rage in Providence just lately. Heck of an upgrade for the Headmistress. I bet Dick Hopewell's eating his hat right about now."

Tony looked away from Josh while Olivia blinked at him like the picture next to the word Innocent in the dictionary. Technically, Tony had sided with the king, but there wasn't a faerie rule about any of that like there was for Kelpies or Selkies. He could switch sides at any time, just like Olivia and Headmistress Thurston. I'd learned that much about the ancient magical shifters since my whole life got turned upside-down.

Being stuck listening to college students again wasn't so bad, even if my feet still dangled an inch off the floor in seats sized for grown people. I was only halfway through being seven. All the same, I wasn't like the regular kids at the school I used to attend. Most of them weren't extrahumans, and none had ever gotten abducted by a Faerie monarch. Being kidnapped was half the reason I had Providence Paranormal College faculty members tutoring me. The other half was my mom getting involved with the wrong ghostly partner and ending up in jail.

It wasn't so bad, especially food at the college. I got to eat sugary cereal pretty much any time I wanted. The mundane history homework Mr. Waban had assigned me was boring, though. But I had to finish it, or I wouldn't be allowed to go and visit Fred. There was already too much to tell him, and this conversation I was overhearing between his friends only added to that.

Josh had called the meeting, of course. The Alpha had about a million questions. How did Tony manage to come back from the dead? Had Olivia always been a magical shifter? Whose family trees had crossing branches? Why hadn't anyone told him sooner about his brother Derek's return?

Tony and Olivia attempted to answer, but the one with the real information was Albert Dunstable. The Sidhe admitted to keeping an eye on most of the Tinfoil Hatters since each started school. Of course, questioning him was a pain in the butt for most of them. Nobody wanted to get in a Seelie knight's debt.

"So, you knew you and Olivia were related all along."

"I wasn't absolutely sure, but I suspected as much." Al shrugged. "My mother always said that her sister was the last Alkonost. I knew we had owl shifter blood in the family, and part of my education included learning how to track coincidence records. When an orphaned owl shifter of the right age showed up here enrolled in the same major as me, I figured there must be some connection."

"Gemma Tolland blindsided you, though."

"Yes." Al leaned his head on one of his hands. "She's always had a way of doing that to me."

"At least you finally stood up and did the right thing by your kid."

"Josh!" Nox Phillips elbowed her mate in the ribs. "It's not his fault that he never knew."

"Yeah, fine, sure, whatever." Josh shook his head. "Trolls like their secrets, but I'm surprised you didn't figure it out sooner, Al. Smart guy like you, big plans with the lady in question. You said you two were set to run off and tithe to the same monarch together, get hitched, and then attend PPC as a married couple. You must have wondered why she didn't show up at school when she said she would."

"It was the other way around, actually. She showed, and I didn't." Al sat up, put his hands flat on the table, and stared at Josh. "Occam's Razor. The simplest explanation is most likely to be true, and in this situation, it seems like she broke a promise in exchange for me breaking mine. A secret baby isn't exactly simple, however."

"I don't care if I end up owing you for asking this, but why did you do it, Al?" Blaine puffed out a couple of smoke rings. "I couldn't have broken a promise to Kim, not even before we knew for sure about our destiny together. Yet somehow, you managed to welsh on your commitment to Gemma."

"It wasn't intentional, I assure you." Al's gaze sank to the table, examining the patterns in the wood grain. "My family had to drag me kicking and screaming to the queen's castle. I imagine, when I didn't show up at the appointed time to meet with the king, she tithed without me, not realizing she was with child."

I tried to imagine a straight-laced guy like Albert Dunstable in full-on freak-out mode. It was a stretch, but I knew he wasn't lying. Tithed faeries, especially Seelie Sidhe, couldn't tell an outright lie when asked a direct question. I almost spoke up, curiosity nagging at me to ask a question of my own, but I didn't want to be kicked out of the meeting. Listening in on my brother's packmates kept me closer to him than I could be without a visit to the Under. I kept my mouth shut, but Lynn Frampton grabbed my burning question and ran with it.

"So why didn't you tell her?" The human's voice was flat, almost emotionless. I knew that meant she was about as angry at Al as I was.

"There was no point." Al closed his eyes. "We can't be together like this, tithed to opposite courts."

"So, you let her stay angry." Lynn's flat voice shook with rage, and her fingertips turned white where she gripped the table. "You let her suffer, thinking the father of her kid is a liar. Like that helps any of you."

Al bent his head over the table as though the weight of Lynn's words pushed him down.

"Lynn." Bobby put his hands over hers, took a deep breath, and then let it out. "In with the Jedi. Out with the Sith."

"Okay, Bobby." She took a few deep breaths and went silent. They all did. "All of this is interesting, but none of it helps Bianca. We came here to plan for that, right?"

Something dropped on the table in front of Al with a plop. Tears. I set my pencil down, about to get up and pat the Sidhe on the back or something. He'd been there for me when I was missing Fred, and I didn't want to watch him cry. But my ability to sit there without being noticed trumped that. If I stayed still, I'd learn more, maybe even enough to help with this whole mess so Al wouldn't have to cry.

My own family, once solid, was now as much of a mess as the Dunstables and the Tollands. I had to try to do whatever I could.

Tony Gitano glanced my way. Other than that, the rest still hadn't noticed me. They argued, half of them dead-set on charging into the queen's demesne to rescue Bianca and the other half holding them back. Tony was part of the latter.

"So we have to rely on people who know the queen." Blaine's nose looked like a smokestack at a smoke factory. "People like Mother, Fred, and Al."

"Al and Fred are just knights, though." Lynn shook her head. "Doesn't give them much sway."

"But Al has leverage in a major way." Kim Ichiro tapped one page of a yellowed text. "He's bringing the queen a major ally. The Alkonost gives her enough magical mojo to get past even the king's power level. Maybe she could be convinced to kick Richard Hopewell to the curb."

"You talk about the kid like she's a powerhouse." Tony shook his head. "Sure, Hope's bonded to that feather, but she's six. I'm not sure that's influential."

"Six?" I slapped my hand over my mouth after the number spilled out of it.

"Hmm." Josh Dennison stood up from his heat at the head of the table and paced toward me. His eyes never left mine the entire time. "I know someone who'd be a real help."

"Um." I blinked, playing dumb. "Me?"

"Yeah, Ed." Josh smiled. "You got big excuses to be in the Under at the queen's castle but can come back here whenever you want. And a six-year-old's going to trust you faster than she'd trust a poison dragon or your big brother the scary Redcap."

"And she won't trust Sir Al even though he's her dad because she barely knows him." I sighed. "Okay, I get it."

"So, will you help us?"

"After I finish this homework, sure thing."

AND NOTHING BUT THE TRUTH

A PROVIDENCE PARANORMAL COLLEGE
SHORT STORY

I hate my son. I ain't a good lion shifter Mob boss no more because his little birdie shot me with her Wonder Woman wannabe truth arrow. So I'm here now, spilling my guts to the FBE's lamest in a Washington DC interrogation room. You know it's true that Natalie Johnson and Derek Dennison suck at enforcing the law because I said so.

The only bright side to any of this is that what I say literally goes because it's no word of a lie. Natalie had dognapped the wrong wolf shifter pup back in the day when she brought Derek in for illegal shifting. Shoulda been his brother Josh; woulda saved me a world of trouble. That son of a bitch kept me from giving my son the punishment he deserved.

And then when Derek came to town and tried to join my gang undercover, he thought I was stupid enough to fall for it. I didn't, of course. Pitched his tail straight into the Under at our first meeting as he deserved. But in the end, Johnson and Dennison only got me because my kid's a rat.

"Tell us how Hopewell met the Sidhe Queen." Agent Johnson sounds like she's asking a girlfriend for hairstyle advice.

"You talk like the dumbest broad since Marilyn Monroe."

"Thanks!" The agent's smile widened, but the light in her eyes goes deadly cold, like Waban's halitosis.

"I don't aim to please."

"I know. You're just doing what you've got to." Johnson adjusts her bangle bracelet. It's one of those magnetized copper deals "As Seen on TV" which doesn't actually work for curing arthritis. But it could put a Roman lion shifter like me into an entire galaxy's worth of worlds of hurt. Or a freaking coma.

"I hate comas." I roll my eyes because that much truth hurts almost as much as copper. "It's public record how they met. Queenie was at Hopewell's and Thurston's wedding, bride's side."

"Gross." Dennison tries to play bad cop and fails miserably. "My father always said you can judge a man by the company he keeps. You and Hopewell must have been bosom buddies."

"We had a mutual understanding, but men like us don't really make friends." I tap my knuckles on the steel table I'm cuffed to, and I want to bust it in half. I can but I don't have a death wish.

"Wow." Derek had a shit-eating grin on his face. I have seen dogs eat that, though, so I can't really blame him for wearing that expression.

"Look, piggies. I can't lie, so there's no point in the Federal Bimbo asking stuff twice or the flaming wolf threatening me." I bared my teeth because I'm way past smiling by that point.

They look at each other. I can tell they've got a mind link going, mostly because Johnson smells like a Psychic of some sort. I tap my fingers on the table, one by one, while I wait for their brains to stop waving at each other.

"Okay, Gino."

"Mr. Gitano."

"Okay, Mr. Gitano." Johnson shrugs with one shoulder. "What's Hopewell's weakness."

"Powerful women." I throw back my head and laugh my ass off and then back on again because I'm actually evading that answer and telling nothing but the truth. That's rarer than I like my cheeseburgers.

"That's not what she means, and you know it."

"Wish I was Fae, so all these questions meant you owed me your lives." I wipe the corner of one eye. It takes a Godzilla-sized laugh to make me cry, apparently. There's a tear there I didn't expect. It stops me cold because I can't remember the last time I cried. Men like me just don't do that, not even when we kill our beloved wives for betraying us or try to murder our punk-ass kids ten times, even if they deserve it.

"Well you're not." Dennison sighs. "We've got to ask as specifically as possible, and I'm not the one who grew up in a faerie family, Nat."

"Okay." Johnson narrows her eyes at me. It looks like a spinster's squint.

"You'll never find a man, carrying on like this, Johnson."

"Huh?" She blinks.

"Hanging out with a gay werewolf." I snort.

"What did you just say?" Dennison grabs me by the collar and lifts me off my seat. I laugh in his manscaped face.

"Gay. Homo. Fag."

"Yeah, and?" His grip tightens. "I'm a wolf shifter, not a werewolf, asshole."

"Of all the things to get bent out of shape over." I shake my head, swallowing the chuckle.

"Put him down, Derek."

"Oh, I wish. Like Old Yeller." The wolf drops me back in the chair and gets out of the way. Johnson sits on the table between the corner and me. I smile like I'm from Cheshire because Psychics are weak. I know this from long experience trading them in like Ferraris.

"You're going to sing like a choirboy, Mr. Gitano." She gives that dopey grin, dimples and all, tilting her head so her brown curls bounce like Shirley Temple's.

I snort. "Make me."

"Oh, but I can. I'm a Telepath."

The smile leaves my face like Tony Soprano on the lam.

"What do you want to know?"

"What's Richard Hopewell's magical weakness?"

"I don't know."

"I guess we can't give you a deal then."

Agent Natalie Johnson stands up, turns her back on me, and heads for the door. Dennison opens and holds it for her, shrugging as he turns to follow.

"Wait." I know it's twenty-five to life if they walk out on me now. That can't happen to a man like me. I shake off the sense that this isn't actually happening. I know from long experience with my particular malfunction that I can't let my ego whitewash the damage, not if I want to see the sun through anything but copper bars and fences for the rest of my life.

"Wait? For what?"

"I can tell you other stuff. About my operation."

"We might just be able to make a deal with you then, Gino." Agent Johnson winks over her shoulder. "But we'll talk about that after my gay best friend and I take five. We'd like to drink our stale coffee in peace, mmmkay?" The broad turns out to be the opposite of dumb. She paces around the corner and out of sight.

"You want some of that crappy coffee when we come back, Mr. Gitano?" Dennison tilts his head up, a sign of concession from a wolf shifter like him.

"Yeah." I understand that Dennison is never the bad cop in this partnership. "That'd be great, kid."

I hate coffee.

The series continues with *Fae or Fae Knot,* coming soon to Amazon and Kindle Unlimited.

CONNECT WITH THE AUTHOR

Find D.R. Perry Online

Website: https://drperryauthor.com/

Author Central: http://www.amazon.com/-/e/B00O6851HO

Facebook: https://www.facebook.com/drpperry/

Mailing List: https://app.mailerlite.com/webforms/
landing/p9i8u6

Twitter: https://twitter.com/DRPerry22

www.ingramcontent.com/pod-product-compliance
Lightning Source LLC
Chambersburg PA
CBHW050336110726
47899CB00007B/2524